# disLOCATIONS

Nine stories of speculation and imagination

Edited by Ian Whates

First edition, published in the UK July 2007
by NewCon Press

NCP 002

10 9 8 7 6 5 4 3 2 1

ISBN:  978-0-9555791-0-3

Cover art and design by Andy Bigwood

Invaluable editorial assistance from Ian Watson

Printed in the UK by The Stevlyn Press HDP

Chaz Brenchley

Pat Cadigan

Hal Duncan

Amanda Hemingway

Andrew Hook

Ken MacLeod

Adam Roberts

Brian Stableford

Andy Bigwood

Ian Whates

*Andrew West* (signature)

Andy West

This special signed first edition of
**disLOCATIONS**
is limited to 500 numbered copies.
This is number:

_____361_____

# CONTENTS

# DISLOCATIONS

## An Introduction

When it came to choosing a theme for this, NewCon Press's second anthology, I felt somewhat under pressure. The first, *Time Pieces*, was very well received, with several award nominations and its cover winning the BSFA for best artwork. That book contains a particularly diverse and entertaining collection of stories and I wanted this one to be at least as original, enjoyable and eclectic.

Then, in the latter part of 2006, I had a conversation with Amanda Hemingway, during which she described a comical story she had written a couple of years previously. The piece features a newly fêted author who ends up floundering and bemused at his first major convention in the USA.

That set me thinking.

The concept of people removed from their normal environment offers a wealth of possibilities for storytelling. Of course, Science Fiction and Fantasy both have long traditions of such tales: the marooned spaceman stranded on an unfamiliar alien planet, a new colony cut off from the rest of human civilisation, people abruptly transported from their mundane lives to a realm in peril where magic is taken for granted and science has never developed… But I was looking for a little more than that.

Rather than retreading familiar ground and reworking accepted tropes, I was looking for fresh and original takes on a theme which has so much potential; from displacement in the purely physical sense: conqueror, refugee, slave, tourist, pilgrim, abductee, guest, mercenary, diplomat, stowaway, etc – to all the other possible forms of displacement: mental, emotional, cultural, political, spiritual and beyond.

I discussed the idea with Hal Duncan the following day over dinner (during which a good deal of red wine flowed, as I recall), and he seemed very enthusiastic, promising to submit a story for the collection. True to his word, Hal duly emailed me his piece some ten days or so later, before I had even thought to approach anyone else. That settled it: 'displacement' would be the theme.

One of the best things about publishing and editing an anthology such as this is that it allows me to approach authors whose work I admire. I did so with *Time Pieces* and I have done so again with *disLOCATIONS*. After Hal, the first people I asked were Chaz Brenchley and Ken MacLeod. Andrew Hook and Andy West followed soon after and by Christmas I was halfway there.

Having drawn such inspiration for the book's theme from that conversation with Amanda Hemmingway, it seemed churlish not to invite her to submit the story in question for the anthology. Then, in the New Year, Pat Cadigan, Adam Roberts and Brian Stableford also agreed to participate, giving me a line-up to drool over.

Eight of the resultant stories are wholly original and most were written specifically for the anthology. The ninth, Amanda's, featured briefly on her publisher's website some time ago and has not reappeared since, so has never before been in print.

When asking this particular group of authors to produce work around a theme of such promise, I was hoping for something special, for stories that would bypass the obvious and would instead surprise and delight me. I was not to be disappointed.

The nine pieces that comprise the final collection provide a richness and variety beyond anything I could have hoped for. All are very different, all fall within the central theme of 'displacement', and all are worth reading purely for their own sake.

Of course, the writers themselves have done the truly admirable part in producing the stories; any credit I might merit is purely in reflection, but I *do* feel a certain satisfaction, perhaps even pride, in the finished volume, as I am sure each and every author does in their own story. My fervent hope is that *disLOCATIONS* will bring as much pleasure to those who discover and read the book as I have had in instigating and compiling it. If it succeeds in doing so, then all are in for a real treat.

*Ian Whates, June 2007*

# Tales from the Big Dark:

# AMONG STRANGERS

by

Pat Cadigan

Six months after the Dacz.va abducted Gloria Muhammad, R.N., from the employee parking lot behind the TriCounty Hospital and Trauma Centre in Cincinnati, Ohio, they knocked her out, stripped her naked, wiped her memory, and left her in the intake pen for carbon-based oxygen breathers at the shelter. The Dacz.va are a whimsical race with poor impulse control, short attention spans, and no sense of responsibility. They drive me crazy.

"At least they remembered to leave her CV," Charlie said as we stretchered her through the concourse to the new arrivals clinic. It was slow going – every carbon-based oxygen breather seemed to be out on a mission today. Traffic was dense and we got a lot of stares, as if no one had ever seen a dump-job before.

"Ought to be in a quarantine box," said a traffic warden sniffily, ruffling all his feathers. Normally I would never endorse a stereotype but feathered bipeds really do think they're a superior life form. The way he waved us past a group of tourists in pressure suits and into the services lane, you'd have thought he was directing traffic at the crossroads of the universe. The tourists seemed to be in awe but they were chlorine breathers from the other side of the Big Box two lightyears away and their weightless environment doesn't have the heavy traffic that we do. Don't ask me why – I'd have thought it would be more chaotic, not less. Go figure.

"Fully sterilized in the pen," I said over my shoulder. "Everybody knows that."

"I don't believe it," he called back.

"Step into the one we just left," I said, turning to grin at him. "It'll fix your mite problem for good."

"I don't have mites!" I could hear every feather on his body going up again. It sounded like a feathery drum roll.

"Stop it, Hannah." Charlie glanced back at me and quickened his pace so that I had to hurry to keep up with him for a change. "You know how I feel about picking fights."

"I wasn't picking a fight," I said, laughing a little. "I was correcting an error that could have serious repercussions. We don't want anyone thinking we don't observe the highest standards of public hygiene. That's how hysterical outbreaks get started. You wouldn't want to suffer through another one of those, would you?"

Immediately Charlie started scratching a psychosomatic itch on the back of his neck. I felt kind of mean, bringing that up – it had been so embarrassing – but I wanted him to get the point. Plus, he drives me crazy, too. Most everything does, out here in the Big Dark. I think the only reason I haven't had a full-on psychotic break of no return is that there's no way I could ever out-crazy the known universe. Not even the small part known to me personally.

"I'd have thought you'd just be happy that the Dacz.va remembered the CV," Charlie said, somewhat reprovingly. He was referring to the band around Gloria Muhammad's left wrist, which contained everything the Dacz.va knew about this human they had abducted. In true Dacz.va fashion, however, this would be a mishmash of hard fact, anecdotes, unreliable observation and speculation – not totally useless but not what we'd have called a CV back in my day on Earth.

"The only reason they remembered," I said, "is I told them the next crew to leave us a mystery guest would be abducted en masse, memory-wiped, and dumped in an intake pen so they could see what they were missing."

"And they believed you?" Charlie was appalled.

"They did. Watch your step," I added as we left the concourse for a narrower hallway. "The orientation here gets variable. I've talked to Maintenance about it several times. They claim they can't find anything wrong."

"That's what they always say." Charlie frowned at me. "You can convince a whole ship of Dacz.va that you can abduct them but you can't get Maintenance to run down a gravity glitch. You are strange."

My translator gave me a little buzz on the last word to indicate it was an approximation. This didn't usually happen with Charlie, even if we were from different planets.

"It's not me," I said. "It's them. Maintenance are a motley gang of techies and machineheads. They get unlimited renewal through their union, so they're probably immortal too, or as good as. They know things that aren't even true yet. The Dacz.va, on the other hand, are like gifted children – very naïve, gifted children. Their biggest trick is abduction. I'm surprised some older, cleverer race hasn't conned them out of everything they own, including their planet, and left them standing in their underwear on some clapped-out moon."

"I think that already happened," Charlie said. "It would explain a lot of their theology. Seriously." He started to tell me about it when there was a funny thump in the air and just like that, he was walking on the ceiling. Despite having to go up on tiptoe to reach the stretcher, he never broke stride. I had to admire him for that. "I'm going to request a copy of the surveillance for this locale," he said chattily, "and then Maintenance can tell me how they can't find anything wrong." He gave a couple of little experimental hops in case there was a pocket of contrasting orientation; if he hit it just right, he'd be back on the floor with me. Unless it turned him sideways. Not ideal but at least it would be easier to reach the stretcher from the wall. "Could be that for Maintenance, this is normal."

It probably was, too. They drove me crazy. They all drove me crazy. Maybe I really was in the midst of a full and final psychotic break after all, I thought. What if I only believed I worked at a rescue shelter out in the Big Dark with a lot of other human races? Maybe I was tripping merrily through the fun house of my own delusions oblivious to a less colourful and more unpleasant reality plodding on around me.

If so, I could have hallucinated a lot less paperwork.

Charlie was back on the floor with me by the time we met Dr. Neep at the clinic. Like Charlie, Neep was a humanoid from a planet other than Earth. Not the same planet – while Charlie could have passed for an Earth human, albeit one a bit hairier and bonier than average, Neep had shiny, red-gold skin like polished leather and a cap of short golden down instead of hair. S/he was also dually-sexed, while Charlie and I were monosexual. I'm not sure whether it was the shape of his/her face or her/his mannerisms but Neep seemed more female to me than male, although in truth those designations were not identical to their counterparts on Earth.

Now s/he hustled us quickly into the nearest empty treatment bay, giving me a quick, sympathetic pat on the shoulder (Neep had been on duty when I first showed up in the same condition). We transferred our new arrival to a full treatment bed and let the stretcher collapse itself and skate off to a storage cabinet.

"Well, will you look at that," Neep marveled, holding the woman's wrist to a scanning plate. "She's from your neck of the woods, Hannah."

The holographic display floating over Gloria Muhammad's unmoving form grew an extra partition to display the data in English for me. "Relatively, yes. She's from Cincinnati. I'm from Kansas City. Slightly different areas."

"Please. At these distances, it's like she lived across the hall from you."

"I suppose." I knew Neep desperately wanted me to be happy that our newest arrival was someone else from my home planet. We don't get many and the last one was a long time ago. But it wasn't going to be as simple as waking her up, introducing myself as her new best friend, and then showing her around. Breaking it to her that she had been abducted on a whim by a bunch of irresponsible joyriders and then dumped to live out the rest of her life in a big box thousands of lightyears from everything she had ever known was going to be an ordeal for both of us – worse for her, of course. Even if she managed to bounce back from a psychotic break in record time, we weren't going to be meeting for lunch in the terrarium for quite a while.

Neep's hopeful expression turned to deep concern. "Are you going to be all right with this?" She glanced at Charlie and I knew she was remembering the last time someone from Earth had been left at the shelter. The prospect of getting news from home from another Earth person – someone whose biology was not similar but the very same as mine – precipitated an unexpected crisis by waking the homesickness I had thought was under control. And Jean-Christophe hadn't even been my case at the time.

"I'm fine, doctor," I said, smiling, and it was the truth. So far, anyway. "You know, I've been to Cincinnati, so it's entirely possible that she and I breathed the same air."

Both Charlie and Neep looked pleased. Breathing the same air has major significance with just about every race I've met out here – every race that breathes, anyway. There is no equivalent that I can think of on Earth, which really baffles me – now that I'm acquainted with it, I don't really understand how we missed it.

"Too bad you didn't stay longer," Charlie said. "You two could have met." Charlie's civilization has strong elements of probability and entanglement running through it. I don't get much of it, especially the latter, and every time Charlie tries to explain it to me, I come away feeling as if I understand less of it than when he started. It's a bit like when I tried to explain the Christian ideas of atonement and redemption. Atonement he understood on a mathematical level but the idea of a redeemer dying to save people from their sins was something he simply couldn't get his head around; still can't. For some reason, I find this rather endearing.

Neep forwarded all of Gloria Muhammad's information to my library and activated the link between us so I could check her status from anywhere. Then she gave her a two-day sedative with plenty of regular R.E.M. – sentient minds react better to waking after prolonged periods of unconsciousness if they've been kept busy.

"Another guest of the Dacz.va, wasn't she?" Neep said. "At least they kept her happy. Or she kept herself happy. Her brain chemicals are exceptionally good. She has the brain of someone who has recently engaged in challenging and rewarding work."

"She's a nurse," I said. "Maybe she had a shipful of patients to look after."

"Or maybe her brain re-set itself when the Dacz.va excised her memories of them?" Charlie suggested.

Neep considered this for all of maybe a second. "The numbers are too high, too strong to come out of her old memories –" S/he paused, looking down at Gloria Muhammad's dark brown face and then reactivated the holographic display.

"Those numbers really are too high and too strong." She frowned at symbols that my translator didn't bother trying to make readable for me. I glanced at Charlie; he looked like he was trying to keep from going cross-eyed.

"We'll take your word for it," I said, chuckling a little.

I knew Neep's own translator buzzed a bit on that one – s/he doesn't really get that idea and I'm not sure whether that's cultural or occupational. "Her brain may be in error."

"I'm not sure what you mean," I said.

"This brain doesn't seem to know that memories are missing."

"Aren't they all like that, until they wake up?" Charlie said. "Even then, they don't know what happened."

"I'm talking about the brain," Neep said, sounding a bit impatient. "The organ. Not what it thinks. Excise memories and the tissue is changed, the neurons, the neuro-transmitter, all of that is changed. But this brain is like one never tampered with."

"Maybe they didn't wipe her memory," I said, feeling uneasy.

"No, they did," Neep said emphatically. "Here is the record." Another collection of symbols appeared. "This was recorded during the process. The memory is gone but the brain tissue itself gives no clue."

"What does that mean for her?" I asked. "Is she going to wake up any differently?"

"I don't see how," Charlie said. "She'll still be in a strange place, unable to remember how she got here or what happened. Even if she knew she had these big, strong brain chemicals, that wouldn't change anything. Would it?"

"I don't know," Neep said. "I have so little experience with this species. For all I know, it's normal. For her, anyway."

"For some species, walking on the ceiling is normal," I said.

Neep eyed me speculatively. "Ever meet any?"

"Not lately."

After Neep tucked the translator under Gloria Muhammad's scalp just behind her left ear, we transferred her to an ersatz hospital room. The decorators had done a good job – the window looked into an area of the terrarium that was thick without being too jungly. They had added a few potted plants inside the room and a vase of cut flowers. Good air circulation and ambient noise as well, everything needed to passively encourage assumptions rather than actively deceive. Active deception never works out very well – tell one lie to an abductee, especially at the beginning, and they'll never quite believe anything anyone tells them. Given the extremity of the situation, this makes perfect sense to me, although one of the other doctors at the clinic claims that mistrust is inherent in all races that use a binary system, especially symmetrical humanoids. Needless to say, I don't understand that reasoning. I would also tend not to believe it, except it sounds weird enough to be plausible and absurd enough to be true. Out here in the Big Dark, weird is state of the art and absurd is the user manual.

While Gloria Muhammad dreamed unawares, I had Charlie take care of my paperwork (there isn't any paper but I use the term freely and it translates perfectly for everyone) so I could spend some extra time checking on my other cases.

The most recent one prior to Gloria was still on her way out the other side of her second psychotic break. Her name came out as Agnes and she was from another planet in Charlie's solar system. Their ancestors had developed local space travel and spread out over two planets. Charlie told us that when he had been abducted, the two governments had been arguing over how to divide the cost of a joint expedition to a third planet farther out. Apparently, they had come to an agreement – Agnes had been taken from one of the pre-colonization teams there after stumbling into a still-occupied landing site. Her abductors claimed her abduction had been an unfortunate necessity to avoid unauthorized mass contact. Said abductors were an amphibious race normally quite reticent who traveled a great deal, migrating for religious purposes. Why they'd been looking for God on a world much colder than their preferred environment wasn't clear but that wasn't our concern anyway. Interstellar travellers answer elsewhere for that sort of thing. No one's really sure who or what that is, not even those who have actually had the encounter. Or so I've been told, anyway.

Charlie was absolutely sure that Agnes's abductors had failed to observe the proper safeguards for an unauthorized contact because they had been overwhelmed by curiosity about her appearance.

Personally, I thought he was speaking for himself. Agnes had been bio-engineered to withstand a cold climate – she was covered with a dense woolly coat like sheep's wool, which, also like sheep's wool, could be sheared and utilized in a number of ways. Charlie was both amazed and scandalized. Bio-engineering had been taboo during his time; his people had changed so much since he had been taken that I was afraid he might have a crisis over it. So far, however, he showed no sign of melting down but just to be on the safe side, I made a point of keeping him away from Agnes.

The case I'd had prior to Agnes was much more encouraging. Tresor was in a re-education program training for some kind of technical work that my translator rendered as a cross between engineering and philosophy, buzzing emphatically on those two words to let me know I didn't have a hope in hell of understanding what it really was.

I felt a bit insulted. Tresor was a very intelligent guy but he'd never seemed like an exceptional intellect. Instead of going to see him, I used my library card to take a deeper look at his records. That wasn't exactly kosher (another word which, like paperwork, translates perfectly for virtually all races) but justifiable, I felt, in light of the rule of perpetual responsibility.

Tresor, I was surprised to discover, had recently been Enhanced. I'd never seen that coming. So much for my assessment of his mental prowess, I thought, feeling a bit stung at not having been consulted. Not that anyone had to – it was just a matter of professional courtesy. But there was no point in feeling bad about it. The Enhancers do their living and thinking Somewhere Else; intangible matters arising in the primary dimensions just don't register on them.

But I couldn't help it. I mean, what was I, chopped liver? The only thing I'd ever been singled out for in my entire life was alien abduction and I'd ended up in a place where that was no distinction. Hell of a thing.

Clearly I'd be better off studying up on my newest active case rather than developing an inferiority complex over an old one. I went back to my workspace to access Gloria Muhammad's records and found Charlie parked in the assistant's pod, trying to look busy.

"I didn't think you'd still be here," I told him. "Was there really that much paperwork?"

"Oh, I was waiting for you," he said, trying to sound offhand and not quite succeeding. "I'm your assistant."

I blinked at him. "You are?"

"If that's all right with you," he added quickly.

I shrugged, unsure if this was a good idea. Having an assistant was the sort of thing that would soothe my still-wounded ego. On the other hand, it was Charlie. On yet another hand, assistant was not actually an official position, so if Charlie lost interest and wandered off to do something else, I couldn't do a thing about it. But on a further and by no means final hand-equivalent, the unofficial assistant job was usually a prelude to apprentice, which was official and which would elevate my status at the shelter.

"If you want to try it out, I have no objection," I said finally.

"Good. I did all the paperwork and I got it right the first time." He gave me a big pleased smile. The smile is one of those signifiers that seems to be universal among humanoids, a fact that sometimes still amazes me.

"Thank you." I requested two seats from my desk; they popped out and unfolded side by side. "Let's have a look at what the Dacz.va left us by way of information on Gloria Muhammad."

Charlie vaulted out of the assistant pod and into the chair next to me like a teenager hopping out of one convertible into a better one. My library had everything cued up so I let him press go.

The holographic display popped up and divided into two unequal parts. The smaller one on my left contained the usual transcribed notes but the larger one was something else altogether.

"Is that a surveillance record?" I stared at the sight of the irregularly shaped Dacz.va bodies floating weightlessly around what I took to be a common lounge area, their many arms curling and uncurling. Still in her white tunic and trousers, Gloria Muhammad was tethered to a couch in the centre of the room eyeing the creatures with apprehensive curiosity while her dreadlocks floated around her head, their movements almost mirroring those of the Dacz.va's limbs. I wondered if the Dacz.va had read more into that than they should have. They aren't totally stupid but I've never met a race yet who didn't read their horoscopes in the morning paper, so to speak.

"I'd call it a home movie," Charlie said, adjusting the sound. It had a cheap tanky quality. The Dacz.va detect vibration. For races who hear by pressing an appendage to a pulsation plate, this is high-end multi-channel SurroundsoundTM. If you have ears, however, it's like a phone call. In this case, a phone call from the birds – the Dacz.va communicate by trilling and they hadn't bothered to put their side of the conversation through a translator and recorded trilling didn't register on our implants. That was no problem – we could do it easily enough ourselves. It was just that the lack of consideration was annoying.

We had no trouble understanding Gloria Muhammad – i.e., the words came through just fine. She just didn't make any sense.

She didn't talk at all until they gave her the headset, which looked like something a telephone operator would wear, complete with microphone. Number please. Is this the party to whom I am speaking? Cutting edge humour in my day. There was probably no one on Earth who remembered it any more. I watched as she realized that the bird-like noises were intelligent communication. But her expression of amazement quickly turned to one of intense, total joy.

"You're aliens!" she said, looking around at them. "You're aliens! Aliens! You are alien people! You're alien people and you're complete strangers!"

Dacz.va body language is not my specialty but even I could see that they were more than a little taken aback by her reaction. This was a new one on them.

"You're complete strangers and I don't know a single thing about you! Not one single thing! Nothing!" she sang and then burst into tears of joy.

I sneaked a look at Charlie to see what he was making of all this but he was busy sneaking a glance at me.

"Ever see anything like this before?" I asked him.

He jutted his chin twice, the equivalent of a head-shake. "Never."

"Any ideas as to what she means?"

"Me?" He touched his lips briefly with two fingers. "How could I? She's from your world, not mine."

"I know. But if she were someone from your world, what would you think?"

"I wouldn't know what to think," he said, suddenly solemn. "Maybe that she hated her life. That she had been miserable among everything she knew."

I scrolled through the print records, scanning transcriptions and notes but there was nothing about depression. "Put in a background search so we don't have to watch this thing all the way through to find out if she ever talked to these complete strangers about being unhappy on Earth."

Charlie did so, then suddenly stopped the movie, backed it up and re-ran it slowly. "Look – she just said something but it didn't record."

"She did?"

He backed it up and re-ran it again. "It was something they couldn't translate even very roughly," Charlie said, "and if it doesn't translate, they don't hear it and it won't even record."

"I don't see how that works," I said.

"Me, either," Charlie confessed. "Something about their clunky technology."

We skipped ahead and found several more instances of cut-out, some rather extensive. In between, there were plenty of getting-to-know-you sequences – Gloria showing them the contents of her purse, the Dacz.va showing her movies of their home worlds and promising to take her to one or another of them. A complete lie – the Dacz.va never took their abductees home with them. Occasionally, they would promise to take homesick abductees back to where they found them but it was a promise they never intended to keep – they didn't inconvenience themselves. Even if they had, so much time would have passed that the abductee would not have been returning to the same world anyway.

"Listening to them lie to her is driving me crazy," I told Charlie. "I think the next time they show up at the shelter, I will have them all memory-wiped and dumped."

"And how are you going to manage that?" Charlie asked, his bony face amused but sympathetic. "All by yourself or are you going to hire an army?"

"I'll think of something."

"In the meantime, let's keep watching this. Maybe there's something further on that will give us some idea of what's really going on."

"You're optimistic," I said. "But even if you're right, Gloria Muhammad's going to wake up long before we get to that part. Unless we get incredibly lucky and just happen to hit it while we're skipping through different sections."

"We could search with a filter," Charlie suggested.

"Sure – but what kind of filter?"

"I'm thinking." His eyes filmed over the way they always did when he was deep in concentration. I went on skipping around in the record and pausing at random places. Gloria Muhammad gave away her uniform in return for what looked like pajamas made out of parachute material, and too much material at that. The Dacz.va didn't say anything about where it had come from; I suspected it had belonged to a previous abductee. The Dacz.va keep a lot of souvenirs.

I found a sequence where Gloria explained emergency room procedures at great length. No sound drop-outs at all in this part, which surprised me, although I'm not sure why. Emergency is another of those universal concepts; so is the practice of medicine and as irresponsible as they are, the Dacz.va are well acquainted with both. A few years ago, I was treated to the unforgettable sight of a Dacz.va sporting a Donald Duck bandage over a puncture wound. It gave me a terrible bout of homesickness; just thinking about it now still drives me crazy.

I had hit yet another sequence of Gloria Muhammad rhapsodizing about how the Dacz.va were complete strangers that she didn't know one single thing about when Charlie finally came out of his trance. "Set the filter to find out what specifically she doesn't know," he said.

"You mean other than 'one single thing'? Which she says over and over and which, now that I mention it, can't possibly be true.

They've been telling her all about themselves. Of course, most of the time they're lying but obviously she doesn't know that."

"All right, maybe that won't work." Charlie slumped, crestfallen and then perked up again almost immediately. "Look, there's another gap in the sound, only this time we can see her face straight on. Can you read her lips?"

I tried, but even in slow-motion and extreme close-up, what few words I could make out weren't enough to tell me anything, even if I had been absolutely sure of what they were.

"It was a good idea," I told Charlie as he slumped again, even the corners of his eyes drawing down. "But there's no telling if I'd understand what she was talking about even if I could hear every word."

Charlie looked at me sharply. "Excuse me but now I don't know what you're talking about."

"What I mean is, I don't know how much time has passed on Earth. For me it's been a personal measure of thirty years. But at these distances, that sort of thing gets slippery. Even if we did breathe the same air at one time, the world she comes from might be no more familiar to me than yours. Or even Neep's."

"But you recognize what she is," he said. "You understand what she does for a living. Don't you? Was there anything in her purse that didn't look familiar to you?"

"There was that silver thing that opened like a clamshell and had what I guess is a telephone keypad inside. And that smaller thing with the little earphones."

"You could probably figure out what they are in five minutes. Less, even."

"If the Dacz.va hadn't kept them, maybe," I said. "But that doesn't mean things still couldn't have changed drastically. Take wheels – they haven't changed in a gazillion years. But the way they're used is a different story."

The discussion went on, becoming deeper to the point where even I had to remind myself to watch the holo display. At some point during a lull, I dozed off. Charlie let me sleep until Neep called to tell me that Gloria Muhammad was finally waking up.

"How is she?" I asked, trying hard not to sound like I'd been asleep myself.

21

"That's a good question." Neep's red-gold complexion had dulled in intensity, indicating she was perturbed about something. "Readings say she's not very happy any more."

"Abductees are always apprehensive when they wake up, if not outright scared," I said.

"No, you don't understand. I said she's not very happy any more. I mean, she's very, very unhappy. Depressed. Miserable."

"Already?" Charlie looked at me. "That's not normal for your people, is it?"

"Miserable just to be awake? Not usually but not completely unheard-of, either. Is there anything significant in her readings?"

Neep hesitated, her colour coming up again. "Yes. But I don't know what it's significant of. If these were your readings, I would say that you were unhappy to know that you're awake."

"I can understand that," Charlie said.

"You can?" I said, amazed.

"If I've had a particularly good dream, I'm sorry to wake up and find out it didn't really happen."

"It could be," Neep said, "but I don't think that's it at all. She's too unhappy."

"I'd better get down to her room right away," I said, grabbing my library card and sticking it onto a flatscreen that could pass for a clipboard.

"Do you want me to keep watching this?" Charlie asked as I went to leave.

"It's up to you," I said. "I doubt you'll learn anything."

"No, I suppose I won't, but I like watching it. I like her hair quality. You people have wonderful hair quality."

That made me laugh. "Thanks. I guess."

Gloria's room was directly below my workspace; all I had to do was sink one level on a liftplate and I was right outside the door to her room. The surveillance feed on my flatscreen showed that the bed had sat her up, adjusting her legs as well to take the pressure off her lower back. The fact that she wouldn't remember spending six months weightless wouldn't make it any easier for her to readjust physically to gravity. I made a mental note to keep her away from variable orientation hotspots until she was good and steady on her feet again.

I saw on my flatscreen that the moment the liftplate touched down outside her room, she turned to look at the door, as if she had seen me arrive. She couldn't have, of course; it had to be a coincidence of movement but it really didn't look that way at all. Very unnerving. I hesitated, organizing my thoughts, and walked in with the usual friendly but vague introductory speech on the tip of my tongue.

I opened my mouth and then just stood staring in silence. Gloria Muhammad gazed back at me, her eyes very bright and wet and clear, like someone on the verge of a fever.

She was in pain, I thought, some kind of terrible pain that somehow wasn't registering on the sensors in the bed. Something the Dacz.va had done to her? Drugs in her food, maybe. That might have been why she had been so giddy over the fact that they were aliens –

"No," Gloria said quietly. "Not because they were aliens. Because they were complete strangers. There's a big difference. And there were no drugs involved."

I felt pole-axed but I was too stunned even to groan. The damned Dacz.va hadn't wiped her memory.

"No, they did wipe my memory," Gloria said, her voice heavy with weary patience. "I'm getting everything from you. And Charlie. Dr. Neep, too, although not so much."

I still couldn't speak. Every time she said something, I only became more confused, to the point where I didn't even know what I was confused about.

"It's OK," she said after a bit. "I really don't expect you to understand anything. You're not going crazy. I'm psychic. Telepathic." Pause. "I hear thoughts."

It took a second or two for the words to sink in.

"I've been this way all my life," she went on, "so I learned how to manage the noise, screen it out, keep it down to a tolerable dull roar. But I never had a moment's rest until those aliens took me. The Dacz.va. The complete strangers."

I finally managed to glance down at my flatscreen. Data was scrolling too fast to read.

"No, I don't remember them but since you know what happened, I know, too. And though I don't remember my time

23

with them, there's a kind of sense memory in my mind, of how it felt to hear nothing but my own thoughts. Of how it felt to be with people –" she flashed a pained smile "– and never know anything about them. The silence." Pause. "The beautiful, blessed silence."

I had to stop thinking, I realized. I was assaulting her.

"Yes, you are," she said, "but it's not your fault. After spending so long with the Dacz.va, I'm not used to shielding myself. And I don't really want to have to do that any more. I know you have so many questions – about what Earth is like now, about why I became a nurse, about why I am the way I am. Your doctors would like to study me and talk to me and find out why I'm the first telepathic creature they've ever encountered. You're pretty curious about that, too, and I have to confess, so am I. But I can't stand this. Yes, I would like some water."

Finally I was able to move. I poured her a glass from the pitcher on the nightstand, stuck a straw in it and slipped the straw between her lips.

"Thanks." She looked down at the flatscreen I had dropped next to her on the bed. "Yes, there's no point in pretending that's a clipboard any more. And I'm sorry you're lonely. I wish I could sympathize it's what I do for a living – but I can't. I'm so sick of you. I've been dreaming about you steadily since your Dr. Neep put me to sleep. You and your life and Charlie and the shelter and all the things that drive you crazy about the Big Box in the Big Dark.

"And frankly, you'd probably feel the same if I could stand you long enough to tell you all about life on Earth since you left. It's no different. The names have changed but otherwise the innocent suffer, the guilty prosper. War in the Middle East, famine in Africa, polluted air, polluted water, yadda yadda yadda, more water, please."

I held the straw to her lips again.

"Thanks. Now listen carefully. Call your Dr. Neep and tell him/her this: I want to be put into the deepest coma possible. No REM, no higher brain functions whatsoever. Then ship me out to the farthest point away from you, to a place where there are no beings who are even remotely human or humanoid. Then wake me up and train me to do something useful. And if that isn't possible, don't wake me up." Pause. "Go away. Now."

Maintenance found a berth for Gloria among the chlorine breathers on the other side of the Big Box. Since they didn't bother with gravity, I figured that would be a double relief for her.

She was long gone by the time the news about her got out. The entire humanoid sector was buzzing about psychic phenomena, even those who had never heard of such a thing. Even the feathered bipeds showed more curiosity than disdain. Because she was from Earth, everyone wanted to talk to me about her. I had a very busy social calendar for a while, so busy that I didn't break down for nearly a month. But when I did crack, it was massive, bad enough that Neep actually called Jean-Christophe, the rationale being that I would be forced to turn my attention to a problem I had already solved.

Predictably, Jean-Christophe and I fell madly in bed again and again it ended badly. But not quite as badly as it had before and we both got over it more quickly. I wouldn't have thought Jean-Christophe would have been an antidote to the trauma of feeling as if I had been cut off from Earth again but he was.

Eventually, Gloria found it in her heart to send me a message about what had happened in the thirty-plus years since my departure. I was unhappy if not really surprised to discover that she had been right – nothing much had changed on Earth, relatively speaking. Not at these distances, anyway. Knowing that drove me crazier than Charlie, the Dacz.va, and everything else out here in the Big Dark combined.

So I suppose I have to admit that I understand how Gloria Muhammad feels, two lightyears away with her chlorine breathers. I appreciate her message but I don't have to be psychic to know she doesn't want me to answer, and it's OK with me if I never hear from her again. I mean, if we have to live out our lives among strangers, it's better that they aren't people we already know.

Pat Cadigan

# PAT CADIGAN

The author of fifteen books, including two short story collections, two non-fiction movie books and one young adult novel, **Pat Cadigan** was born in Schenectady, New York, and educated at the universities of Massachusetts and Kansas before moving to England in 1996.In 1981, Pat and her then-husband, Arnie Fenner, won the World Fantasy Award for *Shayol*, though it was not until 1987 that she made the decision to pursue writing on a fulltime basis. Subsequently, Pat has continued to accumulate both accolades and awards, including the Arthur C. Clarke Award twice, for her novels *Synners* (1992) and *Fools* (1995), and two Locus Awards – 'Best Short Story' (1988) for "Angel" and 'Best Collection' (1990) for *Patterns*. As for accolades, Pat has been dubbed 'The Queen of Cyberpunk', by *The Guardian* no less.

"Among Strangers" is something of a departure for Pat, who seldom writes stories not set on a near-future Earth. Despite having the idea for the piece rattling around for a while, she believes it may never have crystallised into an actual story had the theme of 'dislocation' not been suggested to her, but now anticipates that this will be the first of several 'Tales from the Big Dark'.

Pat lives in Haringey, North London, with her husband, the Original Chris Fowler, her fabulous son (currently working on a degree in sound design), and Miss Kitty Calgary, Queen of the Cats and Everything Else in the Universe, This Means You!!

# CHAZ BRENCHLEY

**Chaz Brenchley** has been making a living as a writer since he was eighteen. He is the author of nine thrillers, most recently *Shelter*, three books for children and two major fantasy series: *The Books of Outremer*, a trilogy based on the world of the Crusades, and *Selling Water by the River*, a duology set in an alternate Ottoman Istanbul which consists of *Bridge of Dreams* (Ace, 2006) and *River of the World* (Ace, 2007).

Several of his works have received nominations for the British Fantasy Awards, and in 1998 *Light Errant* won the BF Award for best novel. Never happy unless he is writing, Chaz has produced a staggering number of short stories in various genres, with more than 500 published to date, some of which, from his time as Crimewriter-in-Residence at the St Peter's Riverside Sculpture Project in Sunderland, were gathered in the collection *Blood Waters*.

Chaz is one of the driving forces behind The Write Fantastic, a group of professional fantasy writers who regularly pool their resources to promote their own work and the genre of fantasy in general. He is also a prize-winning ex-poet, and has been writer in residence at the University of Northumbria, as well as tutoring their MA in Creative Writing. He was Northern Writer of the Year 2000, and lives in Newcastle upon Tyne with two disturbing cats and a famous teddy bear.

"Terminal" represents a new direction for Chaz, being only his second out-and-out Science Fiction story. The first, "Freecell", appeared earlier this year in the anthology *Glorifying Terrorism*.

# TERMINAL

by

Chaz Brenchley

*unspeakable journeys
into and out of the light*

He stood on the Tower of Souls, and watched her fly.

Say it another way, he stood on the high-stacked bodies of his Upshot kind, but that was nothing: filing. Bureaucracy. Paranoia.

It was the locals, the natives, the dirigibles – she called them *dirigistes*, but that was ironic – who had built and named this height, who gave a value to these discards. Black discs, each one identical, each one uniquely coded: each one the residue of a human passing through. A carbon footprint, she liked to say.

At other terminals, other Upchutes, the discards were racked in vaults, in coded order, physical back-ups of what the record said: never needed, simply because they were there and known to be there. What greater security could anyone ask for? Here, they stood in another kind of order. As soon as the dirigibles understood what the discards were, what they meant – in so far as they did understand, in so far as free-floating bags of gas could understand the motives and intentions, the physics and biology of meat and bone, of mammals – they had taken possession, demanded it. They saw humans walk into the 'Chute, they saw them gone, and only these discs remaining; they claimed the discs, and built – well, this. A tower. Tower of Souls, just as they built for themselves, their own waymarkers, their almost-holy statements, *we were here*.

It made sense, he supposed. It was the same message, even. And there was no risk, however much the bureaucracy disliked it:

29

dirigibles were as careful of every discard as the most paranoid could wish. Just, they layered them into a tower, high and broad and solid, mute testament to how much traffic this terminal had seen in its century of standing. The Upshot might not be many, reckoned against downside populations, but they did like to keep moving; every stopover, every staging-post meant another discard, another disc.

This tower was tall enough by now to be a feature of the landscape, standing higher than the terminal roof, though the spire of the 'Chute still dwarfed it. The landscape could use a few features, he thought, weary of endless wind-blown plains; which was surely why the dirigibles built their towers, and just as surely why she flew from here, and why he clambered up behind to watch her.

It was only by grace that the dirigibles allowed it. *Hard-earned grace* he liked to say, but she wouldn't have it so. She said that grace could never be deserved; it came as a gift, the soul of generosity. Like flight, she said, to earthbound creatures; like transit to the Upshot, immeasurable grace.

Even on a low-grav world, flying was still a matter of faith as well as engineering. He always said he himself had faith too much; he believed very firmly in the solidity of things, and the susceptibility of air. She seemed to believe what people told her, and the evidence of her eyes. Therefore she flew, while he kept himself grounded. He watched her soar, and checked her equipment scrupulously, before and after. And talked to her, mid-flight –

*"How's the wind?"*

*"Easy; always easy, this late. Fresh at dawn, but that's fun too. You should try it."*

*"What can you see? Tell me what you see."*

*"Nothing new. The sun's so low, the spire's shadow goes all the way to the horizon like a road, so straight – but you know that, you can see it from down there..."*

*"Not so far. My horizon's a lot closer. And for me it is a road, I could walk it if the sun stayed still."*

*"You do that, then. I'll hold the sun steady, I can almost reach her from here..."*

*"Not so high! Don't fly so high. I told you before, keep the tip of the spire in your eyeline and stay below it. That suit's not rated for heights above a thousand metres."*

*"Well, it should be. I'm fine. Anyway, I can too see the spire..."*

*"Only by looking down. Don't lie to me, I need magnification just to find you. Come back."*

*"Coming! Whee—!"*

*"—Not like that, not all at once! Woman, do you want to see me die here?"*

*"Sole purpose of dive. Ready to catch you when you fall. I thought it would be ironic."*

– because he thought he was her anchor, her tether to the fixities of life. He really thought she needed one.

He thought they all did. So too did the downsiders, legislating for the Upshot community. Set free to roam as far as any 'Chute could fling, essentially rendered into information, they must necessarily be tethered by that same information: a backstory that led all the way, traceable through every separate body, every discard, to the one that they were born with, however long ago. Identity was absolute, and paranoia was the key. If one mind, one personality could migrate from one body to another – and have that body grown specifically for them, to a DNA-weave of their devising – then how could anyone be sure that the person they spoke to today was the same person they were speaking to yesterday? The body might match entirely, but that meant nothing any more. Questions of identity had to be cut entirely away from the physical; which meant by definition that no Upshot could be allowed two matching discards. They called them discards, even while the bodies were still growing in the vats, to emphasise the temporary; and every DNA profile was one-use-only, and whenever someone went through a 'Chute they were fitted into a discard not quite entirely at random. They might emerge as any racial mix and any gender, any body type; the only certainty they had, they would not be the person that they had been going in. If no one looked to recognise an Upshot from one trip to the next, if identity was carried in the mind and not the body, then no one stood in danger of deception. Paranoia was a virtue; people's private codes and passwords were intimate, intense, not to be stolen or given away.

Like all the Upshot, his life was an open book, a matter of public record: how he had been flung out of school, out of the army, out of any discipline he'd tried; how in the end, almost in desperation, he had been flung into orbit to work on terminal construction. His home world wouldn't tolerate a 'Chute downside, but they had the schematics and the skills for an orbital platform, and chemical rockets to get there, and the benefits were too great to ignore. So it was built, and in the building of it he found a life he could cherish. The intimate spaceside disciplines that his and his co-workers' lives depended on; the extraordinary physicality of working roustabout in a suit, in vacuum, in nul-g; the extraordinary physicality of his co-workers in the dorm-ships, inter-shift, where rules and limits seemed all to have been left behind, downside; the constant call, no, suck of the stars, which were not a background to his new life so much as the vessel that contained it.

And then at last the 'Chute was finished, and he was eager in the queue to be away. His original body was abandoned, crushed and dried, compacted and coded by the process that his people had signed up to, compulsory paranoia; he'd been flung far and far, to another planet and another job, building mineworks for a new colony. He might have stayed, he might have found himself a family and another life again. In fact, though, he had been she in that new incarnation. After so long as a male, the shock of change was enough to be dealing with; pregnancy was something else again, and not to be considered. Besides, it was a wild ride, this being flung from one body to another. Why, whyever would he only taste it once...?

So he'd gone on, from that world to another, and another; and like most of the Upshot, he'd acquired the taste first and then the habit of it. And after a while, of course, he began to understand its deeper meanings – functional immortality, to be brief, in a life constantly refreshed by new horizons, new opportunities, new flesh – and he had yet to meet anyone with a good reason to offer, why he should turn away from that.

Here, now, he'd met her, who offered him the opposite.

The suit she flew in stretched into webbing between arms and legs when she spread-eagled, which gave her not quite enough lift to glide in this thin air; even the teasing tug of gravity here would be enough to haul her down to ruin from a height. Extra lift came from the impellers at wrist and ankle. Eventually, with practice, she'd get fine control the same way.

Eventually; not yet. That day she came down fast and awkward, even when she wasn't trying to scare him into a cardiac arrest. Diving she was good at, that sudden plummet where her body was cooperative with all the other forces acting upon it; she was made to fall, as they all were. A steady descent was something else, unfamiliar, unnatural. Unappealing, perhaps.

He watched her come down, said,

*"I don't suppose even you can miss the planet, but you're sure as hell going to miss me. You'll miss the whole tower, if I don't jump to catch you."*

*"So jump,"* she said. *"Take a chance."*

She swooped in, tumbling as she tried to brake and stall and so drop neatly to his side, to prove him wrong. Tried and failed, tumbled catastrophically and would have overshot and fallen thirty metres to the ground, out of any hope of control or recovery. It wouldn't have killed her – probably – and the Upshot always have the option to move on from a broken body *in extremis*, though the move might be unwelcome at the time. Still, he leapt – too high for his own comfort – to catch her ankle, and his weight was enough to pull her down, while her momentum rolled them over and over on that broad platform and they had cause again to be grateful how many of their kind had been this way before them.

When they stopped, where they stopped, she pulled her helmet off and shook her hair loose and grinned at him, sweating and exhilarated. He could only hold to the lean solidity of her and marvel at his privilege, at her trust, at how close they were to the edge.

"You see?" she said. "My chevalier. Always ready to catch me, should I fall."

"Always bruised," he said, "from needing to."

"Yes. Ouchie. Worth it, though. Worth every bruise and every bleeding scrape."

And she was, of course, worth all of that and more. Much more. The Upshot could be as heedless with their hearts as with their bones and bodies, in a life where staying put was stagnation, another life entirely; where moving on – even if they moved together – still meant other bodies on other worlds. It was hard to commit to someone who might be another gender next time round, was sure to be another type, as would you be too. Physical attraction faltered in those shifts, and they were too abrupt to mend in other ways.

He'd never learned to be so casual in possession, of himself or of his lovers. They had been few, then, necessarily; there had been more pain than plenty. Upshot or downside, people mishandled his heart as they did him, mistaking his intensity for passion, his failures for greed. He hurt, and moved on, and took his hurting with him.

It had been a burden, but she freed him. Not of his nature, none the less she delighted in it; and yes, she would come on with him, the two of them together and let the 'Chute fling them where it would, into anything, they could survive it. If she fell, he would be there to catch her; when she flew, he would be there to watch her. One day, perhaps, he could learn to fly himself...

They lay sprawled and sore together on the Tower of Souls, and here came a dirigible, flying above them. Or floating, perhaps, if one could float with purpose. At least some of the time they did that, they had purpose. They couldn't have built this tower otherwise, nor their own.

They built nothing else, that he knew about. Until the first tower was discovered, people thought they only drifted on the wind. Some refused to call them sentient, arguing that they had no more need of intelligence than they did of buildings, engines, any product of mind and work together. Great bags of gas, feeding from the medium they floated in: why would evolution burden them with brains or self-awareness?

Then someone spotted the first of the towers – its shadow, rather, seen from orbit like a needle laid dark and unnatural across the land – and that wasn't a question any longer.

That they had language took longer to discover, and still needed machinery to decode it. They spoke metabolically, drifts of shadow and substance beneath a semi-translucent skin; they needed a day to share a greeting, a month to have a proper conversation. They'd intertwine dangling filaments to stay together, to keep a stray gust from interrupting. Not often, though. He supposed, if you had to reorder your digestion – the closest way he could imagine it – to communicate by gastric rumbles, nothing so simple and convenient as farting, you'd be frugal. You'd save it up. And want to be damn sure the other party was paying attention; repeating yourself would mean going back to the beginning, filling your stomach, starting the whole process again.

So no, this dirigible wasn't going to talk to them, nor them to it. By chance or by intent – he couldn't guess which – it was going to pass directly overhead, and all he could do was watch. Observation of course was interaction, but it did feel a little one-sided. He had no idea whether the dirigible reciprocated, whether it saw him too or how else it might be sensing where he was, what he was, what he did. Somehow, surely; but it had no discoverable eyes, nor any other organ that the xenobiologists could identify as sensory. Precious few organs of any kind, the way he'd heard it. Dirigibles were seemingly careless of the bodies of their dead; after the first few curious post mortems, so were the scientists who studied them. Inside the collapse of the ripped glassine tegument they could trace a few membranes and a primitive digestion, some hint of a nervous system trailing through the fronds, tendrils, call them what you would that hung below. That was all. What fluids, what gases, what more solid masses might hold the mind of a dirigible could still be only guessed at.

A century of study? What was that? It had taken long enough to understand how much the piercing mattered, that they never found a body not torn open.

This one – and if he'd seen it before, he couldn't tell; they really did look all the same to him – seemed to hover a while above them where they lay, though the things moved so damn slowly it was hard to be sure. Maybe it was only caught in an eddy of air, some freak of turbulence caused by the tower or the great spike of the

'Chute behind it. At any rate, he had plenty of time to gaze up at it. The sun on its flank drove light and colour through its skin and deep into the gaseous swirls within, he'd seldom seen so much of mystery; and there was the great dark shadow of a soulstone in its belly, unmissable, enough to make anyone wonder how for so long they had not been missed from the corpses.

On Earth, some birds swallowed gravel and stored it in their gizzards to substitute for teeth. On this world, a mature dirigible untethered from its parent needed some substitute for absent mass, something to keep it upright and manoeuvrable against the wind; and so it would ingest what the first people here had termed keelstones, or simply ballast.

It had needed time, linguists, computers to come close to understanding what the dirigibles called them, which was – or might be – soulstones.

She was quicker to recover from her plummet, his grab, their mutual tumble. Also, she was possibly – no, certainly – less curious about the alien that hung over them, its wafting filaments not so far at all above his face. He had jumped for her; he could jump for this too. He wasn't going to say so, for fear she might try it. She wouldn't think of it on her own account; her attention was otherwise, on him. Her hand was on his clothes, in his clothes, unzipping as it went.

He said, "Don't, not here...!"

"Exactly here," she giggled, "and – oh, here, too. Why not here?"

"Look up."

"I've seen. So what? If it's watching, who cares? Who knows? It can't tell anyone; what would it say? Take half a year, just to misunderstand us..."

That might be true. Perhaps thought as slow as conversation, where it depended on the leak of gases through semi-permeable membranes. Or whatever they did, however they did it. It didn't matter. He felt observed, considered, weighed in judgement; never mind that he couldn't understand the judgement, there were other things he equally couldn't do under others' eyes. Tendrils. Scrutiny.

He pulled away from her questing fingers, hasty to fasten his clothes again. She pulled faces at his back; he knew it, he could feel them. Sometimes he couldn't believe how young she acted. She might still have been in her earliest sequence of discards, barely left home, despite what the record said. It was rare to have come so far and give no signs of being older than your body, not to have picked up even a cynical veneer; he joyed in her enthusiasm, and mocked it, and felt as baffled by her as a dirigible must be.

The way down the tower was a perfect spiral ramp, built into the solid structure as soon as the dirigibles understood that if they raised this thing, people would insist on climbing it. It had taken them a while, three metres or so of accumulated height, to come to that understanding, so the ramp only started that distance above the ground; below was smooth solid wall of stacked discards. In this gravity, three metres could be jumped either way, up or down, but the need to do it amused him every time.

Just as well, when little else in the climb or at the top amused him. She delighted him constantly and disturbed him constantly, kept him on the razor edge of anxiety; sometimes he felt like a parent, having to watch his child fly. Which was absurd, she was older than he was, with a trail of discards twice the length. She didn't like to talk about the past, though, so he never pressed her to it; which made it hard to remember that distance travelled, when all he saw was the bright youth of her body and all he heard was the dizzy enchantment of her voice.

Today he heard that voice laughing back at him, he saw that body a turn below, disappearing a turn and a half ahead; she took the steep smooth ramp at a bounding run, while he walked it like a model of good sense and cursed her in a steady monotone. Even now she couldn't let him be easy, no, never that...

At the foot of the ramp, the flat platform; the jump. And her waiting below, making as though to catch him; and tangling her arms around him, stretching for a kiss and getting it here in the tower's shadow, regardless of whether the dirigible still hung overhead; and walking that long shadow as though it really were a road, for that way lay home, more or less; and walking it hand in hand then arm in arm then closer yet, her arm around his waist and his slung over her shoulders as she tucked herself beneath it: she as shifting, as restless, as physically demanding as he was patient and willing to take whatever came. Willing and wondering and never demanding anything, for fear of losing whatever it was that he had already, her whimsical devotion or her trust.

Home for now, for here was a canister habitat, dropped in from orbit to accommodate the first arrivals, those who built the terminal long ago. It had been his, till she arrived; now they shared it. There was more comfort in the newer dormitories, but he'd preferred the option of sleeping single, a cabin to himself and nearest neighbours a walk away. Now he had her, constantly in his sight, and isolation was another kind of blessing. The Upshot were not body-shy, they couldn't be; when every relocation meant another body and the old one left empty for disposal, shed like a dead skin, what was there to protect? And yet, he wanted privacy from his own kind as much as he did from alien observers; he could never be comfortable sharing a bed in a shared room, in earshot of others.

It was also true that he could never be comfortable with her, in company or alone, but that was another matter. Nothing that she said or did worked to his comfort or content. She kept him nervous, alert, constantly watchful; other people had to tell him he was happy.

She said, "How will we choose where to go next? When we move on?"

He never had chosen, not like that. He stayed where he was until the work was done that he'd signed up for, or until he'd done something so stupid or so graceless that staying no longer seemed to be an option. Repercussions made an effective motive force. Then he'd contact the Bureau and ask about jobs elsewhere, take the first that came available, take the fling.

Now, with two of them, he supposed it would be different. He couldn't even imagine now, what it would be that would make them move. Both at once and both together – how could that work?

He said, "You choose. I'll follow you." There was always work for a roustabout, out on the edge; empires overreach themselves, always, and their peoples scrabble to keep up. But – it struck him, suddenly – what if she chose to go inwards, towards the centre of things, the ancient settled heart worlds?

She was here, though, now, not doing that; her record showed a face turned always to the ever-expanding frontier, as his own did.

She smiled, and said, "Yes. I'll do that. You tell me when."

Which should have answered his own unspoken question, but this was what she did, she taught him anxiety: it might be his to say, but he wanted to please her, he wanted to pick just the right time. How would he know, how could he tell when she was ready...?

He guessed she'd make it clear, when the time came. She seldom did ask a question without having the answer right there in her grasp, held up for him to see it.

The dirigible shadowed them, all the way back. Actually, with the sun so low, its shadow never touched ground where he could see it, but it lingered in the air above and behind them as they walked, in the corner of his sight if he only turned his head a fraction. He wondered if they had curiosity, these creatures: for sure they had some sense of life beyond themselves, that first gift of sentience, or else they would never rip open each other's corpses and salvage the soulstones, to build towers like fingers breaking up out of the soil.

That was all they did build, all the mark they made on their world; grazers and drifters, they needed nothing more. Sometimes he thought he was much the same: he grazed on a world's interest, and then moved on. He left more solid monuments behind him, but that was camouflage, meaningless, the excuse and not the purpose. They intrigued him, with their towers of the dead; something they memorialised, though whether it was the dead or the death or the survivability of stone, he couldn't tell. 'Soulstone' was the best label anyone could offer, it was hard to call it a translation and even that hint of religious significance made him suspicious, but the facts were undeniable. They did salvage the keelstones of their dead, and build them into towers, and revere those towers; they did do the same with the Upshot's discards, to the point where it had needed slow discussion and eventual consent – grace, she called it – to allow people the climb up their own Tower of Souls, to give them a vantage-point and a view across this dreary landscape.

To give her a launching-point to fly from.

Alone for sure, canister'd, contained, with the door dogged shut behind them: here he could shuck his clothes off, peel hers away from sticky skin and make her sweat again before they washed, before they sprawled again in the ruin of their bed and she said, "Low-g, I do love it. When we fuck, we fly. It's so new —"

And then she was abruptly silent, until she said, "New to this body, I mean —"

Which was just as stupid, because they'd been doing it for months now, since she'd first occupied that body.

He said nothing, and she heard that; and turned her back, drew her legs up, huddled herself against him and shivered in their shared heat.

"Who was she?" he asked — which was stupid in itself, because if there was one question he knew the answer to, it was that one. The record said exactly who she was and who she had been.

"You mean, who am I?"

"Yes."

Her voice had shrunk within her, as she was trying to shrink within herself, to be unnoticeable. His arms were around her, but that was a helpless gesture, a mockery of protection. She said, "I was downside, of course, just a girl, but I ran errands to the terminal. For my father, or for anyone who'd send me. I loved it there. I met her, and we were friends. My first adult friend, my first alien friend. She'd been so far, seen so much; I couldn't get enough of her.

"And she stayed, longer than... longer than most of you do. Long enough for me to grow to adulthood, way longer than anyone stayed there, on my homeworld. It wasn't a welcome place to be. They allowed the terminal, they used it for trade, but the Upshot were confined to the compound and none of us were let leave. They said it was our religious duty, to keep within the bounds our god had set us; I think it was political, they thought too many of us would leave if any went. But I wanted, I wanted to go. So much, I wanted it...

"And then she said she wanted to stay. She was tired, she said, and she wanted to grow old in a body she was comfortable with;

and she'd met a man she'd like to make a family with. It was illegal, of course, but she worked in records and her friend drove trucks in and out of the compound all day long. Between them, they could make it work. Except that the Upshot keep such careful track of their people, not like mine; she needed someone willing to be sent on in her name...

"She said she'd change the record, so the machines couldn't see I wasn't her. And of course, once I was here, whole new body, *official* body, then no one need ever know. She gave me all her codes, her passwords, everything. I only had to be careful not to talk too much, about that life I haven't had.

"And I've messed it up already, first world I came to. You won't, you won't *tell* them, will you? You won't tell *anyone*...?"

He wouldn't need to. The woman had lied to her. A terminal's local records could be overwritten, perhaps, by a skilled hand, to fool the 'Chute's internal logs into believing that this body being presented for discard was the one supplied however many years ago to such-and-such an Upshot personality. Internal logs and local records were audited, though. Necessarily, of course they were; and no hand was skilled enough to hide the marks of its meddling from audit. Besides, there was the physical record, tissues taken from the body at time of discard to be matched against those taken at time of issue. Those matches were always made.

She had, how long, a few months more at most? He wasn't in records, he didn't know the frequency of audit. Only the certainty. All the Upshot knew. And that woman had sent a downside innocent into this all unaware, purely for camouflage, a placeholder to distract attention for a while, until authority caught up. She would have known when the next audit was due; likely she timed all this to happen immediately after the last, to buy her the maximum time to slip away with her lover. Planets are large; even a cooperative government might struggle to locate two people who've had time and motivation to bury themselves in new identities far from the Upshot compound.

Meanwhile, this girl, authority would know exactly where to find her. And would come, detain and question. She would confess; she could do nothing else, and it didn't matter anyway. Her body would speak against her.

And then – after how long, how many days of terror and despair? – they would put her in the 'Chute, and send her nowhere. The body would be a discard, recorded, preserved, as they all are; her self would be lost information, deleted, irrecoverable. She'd be dead.

People called them immortal, the downsiders did, but they were very wrong. Everyone dies, in the end. Accident, negligence, deliberate choice: their own, or someone else's.

Everyone dies; everyone lies. He said, "Don't worry, nothing terrible will happen. Just be careful, and don't let it slip to anyone else. You're with me now, I'll look after you." Ready to catch her, should she fall. "We'll move on soon; if we just keep moving for a while, we can leave trouble behind, and give you enough real planets to talk about, you won't even have to remember you've got anything to hide. I promise. We'll ask about work tomorrow, register as willing to transit. Meantime – well, this is meant to be a rest day. Let's do something wildly unrestful..."

So they did that, though she was tearful and needy, so little like the woman that he'd known these last months; and then he teased her, tempted her into showering and eating before he took her quietly back to bed and held her till she slept.

And lay awake all night, deliberately, standing vigil over his beloved; and in the morning, early, when she roused, he brought her coffee and bakies in bed.

When she rose, he had her flying-suit laid out and ready:

"Sun's just coming up," he said. "You could have an hour in that dawn wind you love so much, before we have to get serious. Could be your last chance; when a job comes up, they won't hold it open if we don't go stat."

"Come with me?"

"Of course. When did I ever not?"

She purred at him, and wriggled into the suit's cling. "Promise not to shout, if I go high?"

"Promise to be sensible, and I won't shout. Of course, if the wind should happen suddenly to lift you higher than you were ready for, I'd have nothing to shout about, would I...?"

"I might have to dive quite suddenly too, to correct for that."

"So you might."

So they retraced their steps of last evening, through the clear shimmer of the dawn. When they reached the Tower of Souls he boosted her up to the ramp-platform, though she really didn't need the help, and followed with a barely-graceless scramble.

They climbed the truncated spiral to the broad top, and he wondered aloud what the dirigibles would do when the logic of that spiralling ramp had brought the whole edifice to a point, to match the 'Chute it shadowed.

"Start another tower, of course," she said. "Why not? They've made plenty for themselves."

Which was true, of course, they had; dirigibles had few offspring and long lives, and there were nevertheless many towers. But none of those seemed to be finished, they were all works in progress, waiting on another death. This that they built for human discards had a necessary terminus, and he wasn't sure how they would deal with that.

Still, at least he wouldn't be here to learn.

He checked her impellers and webbing one last time, and kissed her, and let her go.

She leapt from the tower, arms and legs astretch and impellers hissing. She caught the air, or her suit did; seized it, climbed it, conquered it.

Went high and higher, and he said not a word.

Surmounted the spire tip of the 'Chute, and higher yet.

Was a glory, a shimmering speck in sunlight, a mote of something lovely.

Until the impellers failed, all four of them at once, all at the utmost of her flying height.

He had no magnification, but he knew. Her voice would have been in his ears, screaming the news of it, but he'd killed the sound long since.

He knew the moment when it happened, and he knew what she did to save herself; how she spread her arms and legs to use the webbing as much as she could, to drag what little speed she could from her disaster. How she tried to spiral down towards the tower, where he waited, ready to catch her if she fell. He was her solution; surely he would save her now.

How the webbing ripped loose in a second and final calamity, and then she had nothing that mattered: no hope, no steerage, nowhere to turn.

He stood on the Tower of Souls, and watched her fall.

# THE DRIFTER'S TALE

by
## Hal Duncan

Hey, help me out here, mate. You ever seen that show, you know, the one where there's this Chinese monk wandering round the Wild West, just drifting from town to town? He's, like, the stranger that comes into town and changes everything. Ah, yes, grasshopper.

That's it. Kung Fu, that's the one. Fuck, I haven't seen that show for fucking years. Kung Fucking Fu. You're a star, mate.
Well, it's weird. See, I heard they were making this movie and the plot I heard, it was in the present day, but it was basically just Kung Fu. And I thought that's got to be an archetype, right? The Drifter Myth.

Yeah. Drifter Myth.

Well, it's like you've got this guy that wanders into town and... you know, like in that Western where Clint Eastwood rides into town and fucks the local whore and kills everything in sight.

High Plains Drifter. Abso-fucking-lutely.

Couldn't agree more. Fucking brilliant movie.

Well, see, it's the same idea underneath, I'd say. And it's all over the place. I mean, how many books or stories, how many movies or tv shows have you seen with that plot? It's an archetype.

Cliché smiché. Bollocks, mate. It's a fucking myth is what it is.

Well, he's the Drifter, right. He just drifts along, following the Tao and righting wrongs, doing his Highway to Heaven shit or painting the town red depending on his mood. But the thing you've got to know is, you never mess with the Drifter because he always wins. I mean, why is that? That's what I was thinking, you see. Why is that? And you know why it is? You know why it is?

It's because he's the fucking Devil, man. Or maybe he's God. Like, in disguise, you know, incognito. That's, like, a town in New

Mexico, is what it sounds like, eh? Where's God? He's in Cognito, mate. Is that Cognito, New Mexico or Cognito, Arizona? Is –

Ah, fuck 'em. Fucking redneck bible-bashers in here, eh?

Anyway, yeah, so the Drifter is the stranger, right? The Man With No Name. Nobody knows him. You could be sitting at a bar beside him and you wouldn't even know it. He could be me or you. You could be sitting at a bar with me and I wouldn't even know it. Wait, no, that's not right.

Huh? Well, he's not gonna look like Clint. I mean – I don't mean he's literally the Man With No Name, from the movies, like, just...

Oh, right. I get it.

Whatever. My point is, you should know, if you're the local big-shot, never fuck with the Drifter, right? But they always do, and it's always bad news.

Because the Drifter always fucking wins, mate. Always. And the thing is, when you think about it, when you think about it, every culture has the Drifter Myth. Like Dionysus, the Greek god. Sex and drugs and rock and roll, mate.

Bingo! That's what the Romans called him: Bacchus. Anyway, there's this story about Dionysus right, how he comes to this one town and sends all the woman crazy. So the king, he gets real pissed and he tries to trap Dionysus, and Dionysus, well, he gets these crazy women to kill the king. See, he's really come to free the town. He has to drive it fucking crazy first but he's really here to save it. But think about it this way. If you're a tyrant, the moral of the story is pretty fucking simple.

Exactly. Don't fuck with the drifter. But there's all these other mythologies with drifter gods. Sometimes it's the main man, the big cheese, sometimes it's just some little god who has a soft spot for humanity; anyway, he's the one who wanders around and sorts them out, righting wrongs but usually bringing a whole shitload of chaos as part of the deal. Odin does it in Norse mythology. He's like one of those medieval kings disguised as a commoner so he can sneak about and see what things are really like in the kingdom, right, see what middle management are up to behind his back?

Exactly. It's like The Quick And The Dead.

Gnostic parable, mate.

No, really.

OK. You've got Gene Hackman ruling this town. He's the big boss, like the cattle baron in all those old movies. He's the crooked judge. He rules the fucking place, thinks he's the fucking law. He has his right hand man who's turned against him, the devil. And his own son, who he kills. He's the Gnostic demiurge, man; he's fucking God. But Sharon Stone, see, she represents the higher power, the higher law, Sophia. Because she's got the marshall's badge.

Gnostic.

Well, see, the Gnostics thought this world was an illusion ruled over by an evil tyrant god, like the king in that Greek play. Basically they reckoned the god you and I think of as God was a complete cunt, a total fucking –

Oh. Right. I do that sometimes. I'll try and keep my voice down.

OK, so one day, according to the Gnostics, the real god is going to return. He has to come as a stranger so nobody will recognise him, like Ulysses when he returns to Ithaca; he has to disguise himself as a beggar so he can get inside the palace. So he looks like a tramp. I suppose he's a bit of a trickster god, like Coyote, because if you're a god wandering about as a man you've got to be the god of disguise, right?

Both. There's no difference. That's the Drifter Myth at its ultimate. He's not just come to clean up the town or reclaim his kingdom. He's come to clean up reality itself. He's going to kick the fake god out of Heaven, and burn down Hell if he has to, whip the bad guys out of town. He's just waiting for the showdown. But he doesn't look like anything much because he's in disguise. In fact, he looks like a worthless scumbag, a nobody, a drifter.

The point is the Drifter Myth is everywhere. It's all over the fucking place. Every religion has its version.

Hindus? Fucking Krishna, mate. Dangerous little bastard, Krishna.

Buddhism? Who do you think? Then you've got Jesus throwing the moneylenders out of the temple, and – well, they're just all over the fucking place, these drifters, drifting all over the place.

But, I was thinking, see, where do all these stories come from? Why do all these different cultures have the same story? And I started thinking about Homer.

Donuts? Oh, right. I get it. That Homer. That's funny, mate. That's funny. But you know I mean the poet, right?

OK. Well, there's all this mythology surrounding the historical guy, right, like he's a blind poet, he could never write, he just wandered around from town to town, telling the Iliad or the Odyssey in the marketplace. Another fucking drifter.

Sure. I know it's bullshit.

Oh, yeah, I know that. You can analyse the text and show how this part was written in this period, how this other part was written centuries later. Believe me, I know that. But. But, I say, suppose there was a Homer.

Suppose it wasn't a whole load of different guys, just one guy who lived for a really long time. Ah. Never thought of that one, did they? And suppose that's where all those stories come from, all those stories where the guy wanders into town and does his stuff and then wanders out again. Maybe that's just the Drifter God wandering about our world, sitting in a bar in this town or that and waiting for the big finale. Maybe he just wanders from place to place telling his own story in one form or another, making it up like Homer, telling stories about all the things he's seen, but changing them a little bit with each telling because he has to, to suit each particular audience. And that's where all the Drifter Myths come from.

Yeah, but he's like Odin, you see. It's all riddles, all secret meanings. Only somewhere in these stories he drops in his own Drifter Myth just to spread a little truth. He just wanders about spreading the word that one day the tyrant is going to be overthrown.

Well, I guess it's Satan, if you look at it from a Gnostic viewpoint, wandering about the world, keeping his head down but undermining the Powers That Be whenever he can. Lucifer... spreading the light. Hallelujah fucking Lucifer.

I couldn't give a fuck if they're staring. Buncha god-bothering shit-kickers can suck my cock.

Why, yeah, same again, cheers. Heh.

I don't know how far back. I'm trying to think if there's a Sumerian –

Ah... but, of course, you don't have to be convinced. You just have to hear the story and pass it on. That way it spreads, because the story is the Drifter.

Because gods are just root metaphors, right. You heard of memes?

Well, yeah, but the basic idea is just a metaphor for root metaphors, like, 'Time is Money', for instance. The basic idea spreads all through our language: you spend time; you waste time; time is precious. That's a root metaphor. And... but the point is, gods are symbols, archetypes, metaphors. They don't actually exist, but the idea of them is there in a story or a statue. So if you spread the story you spread the god.

Cheers.

Think about it. Right, you're a metaphor, an idea. If someone uses an idea all the time, you could say that it's alive. Not literally, but metaphorically. But if the idea stops being used, it's dead. If it gets passed on to someone else, that's like reproduction. You know the Gnostics talked about the Logos, like, the Word of God, as being a sort of living information. And Jesus is the embodiment of it.

But that's exactly my point. The story about the Drifter carries the idea of the Drifter, and the story drifts, so it carries this idea into every town it pops up in. It's like, all this argument over whether Christ was a historical person or not; it doesn't matter, because his story is the Drifter story, the stranger who wanders into town and sorts it out. And how is it passed on?

Fuck Sunday School, mate. That's fucking bullshit. No. I mean how was it passed on originally. Originally, it was just these wandering apostles, walking about, from one town to the next, and telling people about this guy they once knew. And what happens? We end up with Drifter stories about them, showing up in town, getting persecuted...

Well sure. But if the Drifter is the story itself, it did win. They spread the idea.

Well, mythologically speaking, The Devil and Jesus are basically the same. I mean, Jesus is a pretty transparent version of Dionysus, dead and resurrected, blood for wine, persecuted by the authorities. He's the lamb, the sacrificial animal, same way as Dionysus is the goat... the scapegoat.

Ah, fuck 'em. What are they going to do?

Anyway, Jesus is Dionysus, right, and Dionysus is the Devil, right – horns and hooves, and all that – so Jesus is the Devil. Light of the World, Bringer of Light – Lucifer. It's fucking obvious, mate. It's –

What? Mate, we're having a private conversation here. Do you mind?

Well, hey... forgive me. We're allowed to talk, right?

Well, this beer in my hand and this money on the fucking counter says otherwise, ya wank. What is this? The fucking Inquisition?

Nah, it's alright. I can handle myself against these inbred –

Ugh. Uh, what the fuck... shit... what the... shit, my fucking head. What happened?

Really? How long was I out?

Fuck me.

No, I'm fine. I'll be – fucking hell! What the fuck happened here?

No shit? Sorry about that. I can be a bit of a mouthy cunt when I get a drink in me. Thanks for... well...

No really, I owe you, mate... Lemme get you a drink... uh...?

Fuck, just realised, I don't even know your name.

# HAL DUNCAN

**Hal Duncan** was raised in small-town Ayrshire but now lives in Glasgow, where he is an active member of the Glasgow SF Writers' Circle and an expert on many of the city's drinking establishments. In 2005, Pan Macmillan published *Vellum: The Book of All Hours*, Hal's debut novel, which was subsequently shortlisted for both the Locus Award for Best First Novel and the William H. Crawford Award. The book, with its heady mix of mythology, spirituality and post-cyberpunk SF, and its unconventional non-linear structure, has garnered extravagant praise from some critics and puzzlement from others. Vellum is that rare thing: a work impossible to ignore.

Hal's short fiction has featured in various publications, including *Nova Scotia: An Anthology of Scottish Speculative Fiction* (2005), and the deliberately controversial *Glorifying Terrorism*, edited by Hugo winner Farah Mendlesohn (2007). Hal was first drawn to speculative fiction upon discovering the magazine *Interzone*, his mind being irreparably warped by Ian Watson's story "Jingling Geordie's Hole". Serendipity had its way when, in 2007, Hal found himself the featured writer in *Interzone's* much-heralded 25th Anniversary issue, 209, which includes both an interview with Hal and his debut story for the magazine, "The Whenever at the City's Heart".

Hal's second novel, *Ink*, a follow-up to *Vellum*, was released by Tor earlier this year and seems destined to be just as memorable, controversial and successful as its predecessor.

# BRIAN STABLEFORD

**Brian Stableford** first saw his work published in the mid 1960s, whilst still at school; though it was in the 1970s that he truly hit his stride, producing Science Fiction that made people sit up and take note. His earliest successes included the six *Hooded Swan* books, featuring Starpilot Grainger, a troubled anti-hero whose humanity developed with each new volume. Here was fast-paced space opera subverted, deconstructed and rebuilt according to the author's own unique dictates.

This ability to inject new perspective into the genre has served him well throughout his career, from early series such as the *Daedalus Mission* to the more recent *Emortality* books – an intriguing vision of a biotech future in which immortality has supplanted religion. Brian's work has been nominated for a host of awards, including the Arthur C. Clarke shortlisted *Empire of Fear* (1988), in which a man searches for the hidden truth behind the vampiric aristocracy that has dominated human society for centuries, and the Hugo shortlisted novella "Les Fleurs du Mal" (1994), in which Oscar Wilde attempts to solve a murder in a high-tech future. In 1995, "The Hunger and Ecstasy of Vampires" won the British Science Fiction Award for best short work.

Perhaps the most impressive aspect of Brian's writing is his ability to remain at the cutting edge of his chosen field, as proven by such critically acclaimed novellas as "The Plurality of Worlds" (2006) and "Doctor Muffet's Island" (2007) – both published in *Asimov's* – and his most recent novel, *Streaking* (PS Publishing, 2006), which was shortlisted for this year's Clarke Award. Long may that continue to be the case.

# THE IMMORTALS

# OF ATLANTIS

by
Brian Stableford

Sheila never answered the door when the bell rang because there was never anyone there that she wanted to see, and often someone there that she was desperate to avoid. The latter category ranged from debt collectors and the police to Darren's friends, who were all apprentice drug-dealers, and Tracy's friends, who were mostly veteran statutory rapists. Not everyone took no for an answer, of course; the fact that debt-collectors and policemen weren't really entitled to kick the door in didn't seem to be much of a disincentive. It was, however, very unusual for anyone to use subtler means of entry, so Sheila was really quite surprised when the white-haired man appeared in her sitting-room without being preceded by the slightest sound of splintering wood.

"I did ring," he said, labouring the obvious, "but you didn't answer."

"Perhaps," she said, not getting up from her armchair or reaching for the remote, "that was because I didn't want to let you in."

In spite of the fact that she hadn't even reached for the remote, the TV switched itself off. It wasn't a matter of spontaneously flipping into stand-by mode, as it sometimes did, but of switching itself off. It was eleven o'clock in the morning, so she hadn't so much been watching it as using it to keep her company in the absence of anything better, but the interruption seemed a trifle rude all the same.

"Did you do that?" she asked.

"Yes," he said. "We need to talk."

The phrasing made her wonder if he might be one of her ex-boy-friends, most of whom she could hardly remember because their acquaintance has been so brief, but he certainly didn't look like one. He was wearing a suit and tie. The suit was sufficiently old-fashioned and worn to have come from the bargain end of an Oxfam rail, but it was still a suit. He was also way too old – sixty if he was a day –and way too thin, with hardly an ounce of spare flesh on him. The fact that he was so tall made him look almost skeletal. Sheila would have found it easier to believe in him if he'd been wearing a hooded cloak and carrying a scythe. In fact, he was carrying a huge briefcase – so huge that it was a miracle he'd been able to cross the estate without being mugged.

"What do you want?" Sheila asked, bluntly.

"You aren't who you think you are, Sheila," was his reply to that – which immediately made her think "religious nut". The Mormons and Jehovah's Witnesses had stopped coming to the estate years ago, because there were far easier places in the world to do missionary work – Somalia, for instance, or Iraq – but it wasn't inconceivable that there were people in the world who could still believe that God's protection even extended to places like this.

"Everybody around here is who they think they are," she told him. "Nobody has any illusions about being anybody. This is the end of the world, and I'm not talking Rapture."

"I knew this wasn't going to be easy," the tall man said. "There's no point wasting time. I'm truly sorry to have to do this, but it really is for the best." He put his suitcase down, pounced on her, dragged her to her feet and bound her hands behind her back with a piece of slender but incredibly strong cord.

She screamed as loudly as she could, but she knew that no one was going to take any notice. He must have known that too, because he didn't try to stop her immediately. He selected the sturdiest of her three dining-chairs, set it in the middle of the room and started tying her ankles to the legs of the chair.

"My boyfriend will be home any minute," Sheila said. "He's a bouncer. He'll break you into little pieces."

"You don't have a boyfriend, Shelia," the white-haired man informed her. "You've never had a relationship that lasted longer than a fortnight. You've always claimed that it's because all men are bastards, but you've always suspected that it might be you – and you're right. You really do put them off and drive them away, no matter how hard you try not to."

Sheila was trussed up tightly by now, with more cord passed around her body, holding her tight to the back of the chair. The way she was positioned made it extremely unlikely that he intended to rape her, but that wasn't at all reassuring. Rape she understood; rape she could cope with, and survive.

"I do have a son," she told him. "He may not be as big as you but he's in a gang, and he's vicious. He carries a knife. He might even have graduated to a gun by now – and if he hasn't, some of his mates certainly have."

"All true," the white-haired man conceded, readily enough, "but it leaves out of account the fact that Darren hardly ever comes home any more, because he finds you as uncomfortable to be with as all the other men who've briefly passed through your wretched life. To put it brutally, you disgust him."

"Tracy loves me," Sheila retorted, feeling far greater pressure to make that point than to ask the man with the briefcase how he knew Darren's name.

The briefcase was open now, and the tall man was pulling things out at a rate of knots: weird things, like the apparatus of a chemistry set. There were bottles and jars, flasks and tripods, even a mortar and pestle. There was also something that looked like a glorified butane cigarette lighter, whose flame ignited at a touch, and became more intense in response to another.

"That's true too," her remorseless tormentor went on. "There's a lot of love in Tracy, just as there was always a lot of love in you, always yearning for more and better outlets. She can't hang on to relationships either, can she? She hasn't given up hope yet, though. Darren wouldn't be any use, because the mitochondrial supplement atrophies in males long before they reach puberty, but I could have gone to Tracy instead of you, and would probably have found her more cooperative. It wouldn't have been sporting, though. She's still a child, and you're entitled to your chance. It wouldn't be fair simply to pass you over. Her life will change irrevocably too, once you're fully awake. So will Darren's, although he probably won't be quite as grateful."

That was too much. "What the fuck are you talking about, you stupid fuck?" Sheila demanded, although she knew that he would see that she was cracking up, that he had succeeded in freaking her out with his psychopathic performance.

"My name – my true name, not the one on my driving licence – is Sarmerodach," the tall man said. "This body used to belong to an oceanographer named Arthur Bayliss, PhD, but I was able to rescue him from an unbelievably dull life wallowing in clathrate-laden ooze. The predatory DNA that crystallized in my viral avatar dispossessed his native DNA, little by little, in every single cell in his body, and then set about resculpting the neuronal connections in his brain. The headaches were terrible. I wish I could say that you won't have to suffer anything similar, but you will – not for nearly as long, but even more intensely. I wish it were as simple as feeding you a dose of virus-impregnated ooze, but it isn't. Your predatory DNA is already latent in your cells, secreted in mitochondrial supplements, awaiting activation. The activation process is complex, but not very difficult if you have the right raw materials. I have – although it wasn't easy to locate them all. It will take an hour to trigger the process, and six months thereafter to complete the transition."

Sheila had hardly understood a word of the detail, but she thought she had got the gist of the plan. "Transition to what?" she asked, thinking of the Incredible Hulk and Mr Hyde.

"Oh, don't worry," he said. "You'll still look human. Your hair will turn white overnight, but you'll be able to watch the flab and the cellulite melt away. You won't look like a supermodel, but you will live for thousands of years. In a sense, given that the real you is locked away in your mitochondrial supplements, you already have. Your other self is one of the Immortals of Atlantis."

Sheila had always felt that she was fully capable of dealing with psychopaths – she knew so many – but she knew from bitter experience that negotiating with delusional schizophrenics was a different kettle of fish. She started screaming again, just as loudly and even more desperately than before.

In all probability, she thought, there would be at least a dozen people in the neighbouring flats who could hear her. The chances of one of them responding, in any way whatsoever, were pretty remote – screaming passed for normal behaviour in these parts – but it might be her last hope.

Arthur Bayliss, PhD, alias Sarmerodach, obviously thought so too, because he crammed a handkerchief into her open mouth and then used more of his ubiquitous cord to make a gag holding it in place.

Then he got busy with his chemistry set.

Sheila had no idea what the ingredients were that her captor was mixing up in his flasks, but she wouldn't have been at all surprised if she'd been told that they included virgin's blood, adder's venom and the hallucinogenic slime that American cane toads were rumoured to secrete. There were certainly toadstool caps, aromatic roots and perfumed flowers among the things he was grinding up in the mortar, and Sheila was prepared to assume that every one of them was as poisonous as deadly nightshade and as dangerous to mental health as the most magical magic mushrooms in the world.

The tall man talked while he worked. "I'd far rather observe the principle of informed consent," he said, "even though I'm not really a PhD any more, let alone a physician, but it's not really practical in the circumstances. Your false self would be bound to refuse to realise your true self, no matter how worthless a person you presently are or how wretched a life you presently lead, because selves are, by definition, selfish."

He paused to deploy a spatula, measuring out a dose of red powder. He tipped it into the flask whose contents were presently seething away over the burner. He didn't use scales, but the measurement was obviously delicate.

"If caterpillars had the choice," he continued, "they'd never consent to turn into butterflies. Some kinds of larvae don't have to, you know – it's called paedogenesis. Instead of pupating and re-emerging as adults they can grow sex organs and breed as juveniles, sometimes for several generations. They still transmit the genes their descendants will eventually need to effect metamorphosis, though, in response to the appropriate environmental trigger, so that those descendants, however remote, can eventually recover their true nature, their true glory and their true destiny."

He paused again, this time to dribble a few drops of liquid out of the mortar, where he'd crushed a mixture of plant tissues, into a second flask that had not yet been heated at all.

"That's what the Immortals of Atlantis did," he went on, "when they realised that they were about to lose all their cultural wealth once their homeland disappeared beneath the sea. They knew that the next generation, and many generations thereafter, would have to revert to the cultural level of Stone Age barbarians and take thousands to years to achieve a tolerable level of civilization, but they wanted to give them the chance to become something better, when circumstances became ripe again. So the Immortals hid themselves away, the best way they could. The Atlantean elite were great biotechnologists, you see; they considered our kind of heavy-metal technology to be inexpressibly vulgar, fit only for the toilsome use of slaves."

This time he stopped to make a careful inspection of some kind of paste he'd been blending, lifting a spoonful to within a couple of inches of his pale grey eyes. He didn't have a microscope either.

"What would our elite do, do you think," he resumed, "if the Antarctic ice melted and the sea swamped their cities, and the methane gushing out of the suboceanic clathrates mopped up all the oxygen and rendered the air unbreathable? I think they'd retreat underground, burrowing deep down and going into cultural hibernation for a thousand or a hundred thousand years, until the ever-loyal plants had restored the breathability of the atmosphere again. But that's not going to happen, because you and I — and the other Immortals, when we've located and restored a sufficient number — are going to see that it doesn't. We'll have the knowledge, once you're fully awake, and we'll have the authority. The only way the world can be saved is for everyone to work together and do what's necessary, and that isn't going to happen unless someone takes control and reinstitutes a sensible system of slavery. The Immortals will be able to do that, once we've resurrected enough of them. This is just the beginning."

He took one flask off the burner and replaced it with another; the pause in his monologue was hardly perceptible.

"As you might be able to see," he said, gesturing expansively to take in all the different compounds he was making up, "the process of revitalization has five stages – that's five different drugs, all of them freshly-prepared to very specific recipes, administered in swift sequence. Don't worry – it doesn't involve any injections, or even swallowing anything with a nasty taste. All you have to do is breathe them in. It's even simpler than smoking crack. I know it looks complicated, and it could all go wrong if I made the slightest mistake in the preparation or administration, but you have to trust me. Dr Bayliss has never done anything like this before, but Sarmerodach has. He hasn't lost the knack, even though he's spent the last few thousand years lying dormant in the suboceanic ooze encoded as a crystalline supervirus. Everything's just about ready. You mustn't be afraid, Sheila, you really..."

He stopped abruptly as the doorbell rang. For a second or two he seemed seriously disconcerted – but then he relaxed again. He knew her children's names, and more about her than anyone had any right to know, He knew that she never answered the doorbell.

For the first time in her life, Shelia yearned to hear the sound of someone kicking the door in, splintering the wood around the lock and the bolts.

Instead, she heard several sets of shuffling footsteps moving away from the flat. If she'd screamed then it might just have made a difference, but she couldn't.

"Good," said the man with the PhD. "We can get on with the job in peace."

The first drug, which the tall man administered simply by holding a loaded spoon beneath her nostrils, made Sheila feel nauseous. It wasn't that it stank – its odour was delicately sweet, like the scent of sugared porridge heating up in the microwave – but that it disturbed her internal equilibrium in a fashion she'd never experienced before.

The second, which he administered by pouring warm liquid on to cotton wool and holding it in the same position, disturbed her even more profoundly. At first, it just tickled – except that she'd never been tickled inside before, in her lungs and liver and intestines instead of her skin. Then the tickling turned into prickling, and it felt as if a thorn-bush were growing inside her, jabbing its spines into every last corner of her soft red flesh. She hadn't known that it was possible to endure such agony without being rendered unconscious by shock and terror.

"Just be patient," he said, infuriatingly. "It will pass. Your cells are coming back to life, Sheila. They've been half-dead for so long – much longer than your own meagre lifetime. A metazoan body is just a single cell's way of making more single cells, you see; sex and death are just means of shuffling the genetic deck, so that cells are capable of evolution. All metazoan cells are partly shut down – they have to be, to specialise them for specific physiological functions – but they can all be reawakened, wholly or partially, by the right stimulus."

The pain abated, but not because her captor's voice had soothed it away. It abated because the second drug had now completed its work, having been scrupulously ferried to every hinterland of her being by her dutiful bloodstream. It had taken time, but that phase was finished.

Sheila felt better, and not just in the way she usually felt better after feeling ill or depressed, which was only a kind of dull relief, comparable to that obtainable by such proverbial means as ceasing to bang one's head against a brick wall. She actually felt better, in a positive sense. It was a very strange sensation, by virtue of its unfamiliarity – but there were still three drugs to go.

The ex-PhD had been measuring her condition with his uncannily skilful eyes. He had to get the timing right, but he was as adept at that as he had been at the mixing and the cooking. He had the third compound ready, and he lifted the whole flask up and swirling its contents around to make the vapour rise up from its neck.

This time, the effect was narcotic, or at least anaesthetic. Sheila felt that she was falling asleep, but she didn't lose consciousness, and she didn't begin to dream. It was a little like getting high, albeit more in the crystal meth vein than a heroin kick, but it was quite distinct. For one thing, it didn't seem that she was only feeling it in her head, or in her nerves. It seemed that she was feeling it in every organic fibre of her being, and then some. It made her feel much bigger than she was, and much more powerful – but not, alas, powerful enough to break the bonds that held her tight to the chair. The anaesthetic effect wasn't dulling, or straightforwardly euphoric, but something that promised to take her far beyond the reach of pain.

It was, alas, flattering only to deceive. It hadn't taken her beyond the reach of pain at all, but merely to some existential plane where pain came in different, previously unknown forms. The fourth drug – the first one whose vapour was hot enough to scald the mucous membranes of her nasal passages and bronchi – was a real bastard. It gave her the migraine to end all migraines, visual distortions and all; it plunged a million daggers into her flesh; it sent waves of agony rippling through her like sound-waves, as if she were imprisoned in a gigantic church bell smashed by a sequence of steel hammers – but the vibrations were silent, even though she hadn't gone deaf.

She could still hear Sarmerodach rambling on, and make out every word in spite of her excruciation.

"You'll begin to feel more yourself soon," he said. "You'll begin to feel Sheila slipping away, like the husk of a redundant cocoon. You'll be able to sense your true being and personality – not well enough for a while to put a name to yourself, but well enough to know that you exist. You'll be able to catch glimpses of the possibilities inherent within you – not just the power but the aesthetic sensibility, the awareness of the physiological transactions of hormones and enzymes, the ecstasy of the mitochondria and the triumph of the phagocytes. The agony is just a kind of birth-trauma, a necessary shock. As it fades, you'll begin to sense what you truly are, and what you might eventually..."

The last word of the sentence died on his thin lips as the doorbell sounded again. This time, the repeated ring was swiftly followed by the sound of fists pounding on the door. No one shouted "Police!" though – what they shouted instead was: "Darren! We know you're in there!"

The boys at the door didn't have Sarmerodach's uncanny powers of intuition. What they thought they 'knew' was utterly false. Wherever Darren was hiding, it wasn't at home.

As the white-haired man reached for his spoon again, with a hand that had begun, ever so slightly, to tremble, the sound of thumping fists was replaced by the sound of thudding boots. The door had far too little strength left in it to resist for long. It splintered, and crashed against the hallway wall.

Sarmerodach was already holding the spoon up to Sheila's nose. Wisps of vapour were already curling up into her nostrils. She could already sense its exotic odour – which she normally wouldn't have liked at all, but which somehow seemed, at this particular moment, to be the most wonderful scent she'd ever encountered.

Time seemed to slow down. The sitting room door burst open in slow motion, and the boys stumbled through the doorway in a bizarrely balletic fashion, floating with impossible grace as they got in one another's way. Only one of them had a gun, but the other three had knives, and all four were ready for action.

There was something irredeemably comical about the way they stopped short as they caught sight of the scene unfolding before their eyes. Their jaws dropped; their eyes seemed actually to bulge.

Under normal circumstances, of course, they'd have threatened Sheila with their weapons. They'd have threatened to hit her, and then they would probably have slashed her face, not because she was being uncooperative in refusing to tell them where Darren was, but simply because they were pumped up and incapable of containing their violence. They might even have raped her, and told themselves afterwards that they were 'teaching Darren a lesson' – but when they saw her tied up and helpless, apparently being threatened by a man in a suit, if only with a spoon, a different set of reflexes kicked in. Suddenly, Sheila was one of their own at the mercy of a feral bureaucrat.

Somehow, the tall man had crossed the estate with his briefcase without attracting sufficient attention to be mugged, but he wasn't inconspicuous any more.

The members of the pack hurled themselves upon the outsider. At first, they probably only intended to kick the shit out of him – but three of them were wielding knives. The one with the gun never fired it; he, at least, still had a vestige of self-restraint. The others were not so intimidated by the talismanic power of their own armaments.

The killing would probably have qualified as manslaughter rather than murder, even if it hadn't seemed to its perpetrators to be a clear case of justifiable homicide; not one of the boys was capable of formulating an intention to kill within the very limited time at their disposal. Even so, the tall man was doomed within a matter of seconds – down and out in ten, at the most, and well on his way to extinction after forty, by which time his heart had presumably stopped and his brain was no longer getting sufficient oxygen to function.

The spoon flew from his hand and disappeared from view, taking its cargo of aromatic pulp with it.

Sheila had been saved, in the proverbial nick of time. If the spoon had been held in place for ten seconds more...

Sheila really had been saved, and she knew it. If she had breathed in the prescribed dose of the fifth perfume, she would have ceased to be herself and would have begun an inexorable process of becoming someone else.

She never believed, even momentarily, that she would actually have become one of the Immortals of Atlantis, ready to take command of her faithful slaves and restore her sisters to life, in order that they could take over the world and save humankind from self-destruction by means of benevolent dictatorship. She wasn't that mad... but she knew that, however crazy or deluded Sarmerodach had been, he had been dead right about one thing. She wasn't really the person she thought she was, and never had been. There really was a flab-free, cellulite-free, thinking individual lurking somewhere inside her, in the secret potentialities of her cellular make-up – a person who might have been able to get out, if only four pathetic rivals of Darren's equally pathetic gang hadn't decided that it was his turn to be taken out in their lame and stupid drug-war.

Sheila had no idea who that latent person might have been. She certainly couldn't put a name to her. One thing she did know, though, without a shadow of lingering doubt, was that all that hideous pain would somehow have been worthwhile, if only she'd been able to complete the ritual.

It was a ritual, she decided, even though it really was some kind of occult science, and not mere magic at all. It was an initiation ceremony: a symbolic process of existential transition, like marriage or graduation, but a million times better and more accurate.

Whether she had turned out to be one of the Immortals of Atlantis or not, Sheila knew that she would have become somebody. She would have become a butterfly-person instead or a caterpillar-person – or maybe, even better, a dragonfly-person or someone equipped with a deadly sting. She had not seen anything distinctly when she had sucked those first few wisps of vapour number five avidly into her aching lungs, but she had felt such a yearning for sight as she had never conceived before, or ever thought conceivable – and still did.

But she had lost the opportunity, probably forever.

When the police eventually turned up, in the wake of the ambulance she summoned to dispose of the body, she told them what had happened. She didn't identify the boys, of course, but it didn't take long for the police to figure out who had done what to whom, and why. When all the statements had been collected, all the stories matched – which made the police furious, because they really wanted to put the boys away for something meatier than possession of illegal weapons, and Sheila too – for perverting the course of justice, if nothing else – but they knew that they wouldn't be able to make anything heavy stick, even though the victim had once been a respectable oceanographer before he had flipped his lid and gone round the bend.

In the end, the body was taken away. Sheila was kicked out of the flat, because it was a crime scene, and because the bloodstains and all the "miscellaneous potentially toxic contaminants" would need the careful attention of a specialist cleaning-squad before the council could 'deem it fit for re-habitation'. Darren couldn't be found, but social services managed to locate Tracy so that she could be 'temporarily rehoused', along with her mother, in a single room in a rundown B&B.

In the twenty minutes or so before Tracy skipped out again to find somewhere less suitable to sleep, Sheila gave her a big hug.

"There's no need to worry about me, love," she said, unnecessarily. "I'm okay, really I am. But I want you to know, before you go, that I love you very much."

There was, of course, much more that she might have said. She might have said that she also wanted her daughter to know that she was the flesh of her flesh, and that it was very special flesh, and that if ever a mysterious man came into her life who'd been messing about with ooze dragged up from the remote ocean bed, and had picked up some sort of infection from it that had driven him completely round the twist, then maybe she should show a little patience, because it would probably be Sarmerodach, reincarnate again and trying heroically to fulfil his age-long mission, just like the freak in bandages from The Mummy, but in a smoother sort of way. She didn't, of course. That would have been ridiculous, and Tracy wouldn't have taken a blind bit of notice.

Once Tracy had gone, though, and Sheila was alone in her filthy and claustrophobic room, with the TV on for company but not really watching it, she couldn't help wondering whether there might be a glimmer of hope, not just for her and Tracy, or Darren, but for the whole ecocatastrophe-threatened world.

She decided, eventually, that she might as well believe that there was.

Brian Stableford

# THE GLASS FOOTBALL

by

Andrew Hook

I don't think we ever meant to kick her. It was just something that happened. One of those things that you tend to slide into when you're at school. One moment you're in the right group, then you're in the wrong group. Then someone's down on the floor and there's a boot going in. It was just that one time it happened to be a girl. Whether she went down by mistake, or we pushed her, or whatever; there she was and my right boot was heading towards her face. Amazingly, no one grassed. I'd probably forgotten about it by the end of the week. No doubt it took Melanie longer, but surely she would have done so eventually.

Dermot never entered rooms, he bled into them. One moment he wouldn't be there, and then, slowly, like watching the minute hand on a clock, he would be. You could only track his presence by comparing where he was to where he had been.

If this sounds confusing, then that's because it is. Dermot was someone short of an identity. He had no presence until he segued into that of others. He was the pause between one song finishing and the other song starting. I always wondered why he came to parties at all.

Emma had the same opinion, except with one major difference. She fancied him.

There was a student party in a small terrace off Unthank Road that we gate-crashed one evening, Emma and I on our way back from The Lily Langtry after a night of friendly drinks. The front door was partly open, and Emma seemed to think that she knew who lived there, but as it turned out she didn't, although that was of no consequence. A Nouvelle Vague CD was winding down the

67

evening, their version of 'Dancing with Myself' playing as we entered the room. At first we couldn't see anyone we knew, but after a while we spotted Dermot in the corner of the room. He was smoking, looking bored, talking to no one.

We'd managed to find ourselves a place on a tattered sofa that had accumulated wine stains in a Rorschach test pattern. It sank in the middle, so we were squashed together shoulder to shoulder and we weren't going to move. Someone lent us a corkscrew for the bottle of red we'd bought from the off-licence after leaving the pub, and we took turns swigging from it. A couple of girls were in the centre of the room, dancing to the music, their skirts swirling around the tops of their knees. Emma nudged my elbow. I thought she'd noticed I was watching them, but instead she nodded across to Dermot. He'd finished his cigarette, but its absence was the only indication that he'd moved.

I fancied Emma something rotten, of course. I think she knew it, but we went under the pretence of only being friends. Another night she'd told me Dermot attracted her, but I was sober then. Now I said: "What do you see in him, anyway?"

"Nothing," she said. "Which is exactly why I like him."

I'd always found Dermot hard to describe and Emma's opinion didn't add much either. Sometimes I'd say that I could describe him only by discounting what he wasn't. Once you'd gone through all the physical, emotional, spiritual elements you could think of, then what was left would be Dermot. No one I ever knew had managed to have a deep conversation with him. He was as shallow as the reflection of a ghost.

And yet, unlike even a ghost, he was always there. Always invited, always in the newsagents when you popped in for the packet of fags you'd promised to give up, always at your shoulder in the pub just before buying a round. He was like a visible invisible man.

He wasn't just simply tolerated. Sometimes I thought it might only be me – that I singled him out because I knew Emma had a thing for him and it annoyed me – but once I became aware of his almost unnatural presence I could watch how others interacted with him. And most often, apart from an Alright Dermot at the start of the evening when he would appear at the fringes of the group, they didn't.

We fell asleep on the sofa that particular evening, the dregs of our wine bottle adding to the reddy-purple colour swirl. Dermot had left at some point during the evening, but neither Emma nor I noticed him go. One moment he was there, then he wasn't.

Emma did her best to court him, and – rather infuriatingly as it was me I wished she'd turn her attention to – she let me in on every detail. He wasn't shy, she said, he was a step removed from that. And he wasn't melancholy, as some had said – either genuinely or like the faux-goths that hung around outside the library in their designer-vampish clothes – although he didn't laugh at her jokes. Rather, and this was the best way that she could phrase it, he was symbiotic. Not in a parasitical sense, but in a way which led to connections. When she was with him, she felt whole. Just as a party only seemed to come alive when he was present. He added nothing, except completion.

I never asked her if they slept together. Eventually, after some persuasion, Emma turned her attentions to me. We did the usual things. Made each other laugh, had sex, eventually moved in with each other and got married. But even after having children there was still something that was missing. I loved Emma and she loved me. However this wasn't enough. We hardly saw Dermot at all, but when we did I always felt myself reaching for Emma's hand.

I never planned for it to happen. I was travelling across to Peterborough and she was on the same train. I hadn't taken the car because it had almost failed the MOT and the garage wanted to keep it in overnight. I hate those courtesy cars they fob off on you; it takes me a while to get used to them and when you return to your own car it never quite feels the same. In a way, it was similar to how it might feel if I were to sleep with Emma immediately after having an affair. The difference would be in my head, even if outwardly nothing had changed.

Perhaps this seems a crude analogy, but in this case it's pertinent because on that train journey I met Melanie again.

Some fifteen years had passed since I'd kicked her in the face, but I recognised her immediately. Although she'd obviously filled out in all the right places, it seemed that those additions had simply been hung onto her existing frame. She certainly didn't look as old as me, and whilst her nose appeared a little crooked from where I'd broken it, this only added something to her face. She seemed sexier because of it.

There was one of those immobile tables between us, and my seat faced the direction we were travelling. The other two seats were occupied by the time Melanie boarded, and in fact the train shuddered and began to move as she scanned and re-scanned her ticket. It took her a while, but eventually she asked me if I could swap seats with her.

"I can't travel backwards," she said with a smile.

I returned her smile and we changed seats. Maybe she did recognise me then, I don't know. But what I do know is from that point onwards she was always travelling forwards and I was always going backwards.

We fell to talking on the journey. Technically, I'd some work to do on the train for the business meeting I was attending, but I knew the presentation inside out as I'd done it several times before. Melanie pulled a fat Harry Potter out of her bag, but like an anorexic with a salad she never really seemed to touch it. Just dipped into it occasionally, turned her face to the window, and turned her face to me.

We slipped into an easy conversation, although I was careful not to say that I remembered her. She was incredibly attractive, possessing a hint of dark sexuality, with her face framed by long black hair that curled in towards her neck where an Adam's apple would be on a man. I tried to remember if I'd fancied her at school, but the details were hazy. All that came to mind were groups of girls giggling in packs, none of them distinguishable. My main memory was when she was down on the floor. Her eyes frightened, yet also brimming with acceptance. I asked her whether she lived in Peterborough, Norwich, or somewhere in between.

"I've always lived in Norwich," she said, as if it was a surprise that we had never bumped into each other. By the end of the train journey we'd established that I was married and she was single. I don't know whether it was because I'd told a few lies about the marriage, or whether she appreciated those moments which were obviously the truth, but when we left the train we took each other's hands and crossed the road into the Great Northern Hotel opposite the station. It was an antiseptic building, but so, in a way, was the sex.

I ignored the welts that rippled across Melanie's back as I fucked her, the cigarette burns on her upper arms, and the track marks that I thought I could discern in the half-light from the bedside lamp. She wanted me to slap her, and I drew my hand back for what seemed like forever before bringing it down upon her arse. After that first time, it was easy.

I had to get a taxi to the meeting, even though it was only fifteen minutes walk up Bright Street. Even then I was almost late, and I thanked God that I knew the presentation inside out. My mouth was on autopilot, my penis was sore from the sex and the position it lay in after I'd stuffed it back into my pants, but I was buzzing. Buzzing like I'd never buzzed before.

On the train back to Norwich I saw Dermot. He was in the seat in front of me. I could only see the back of his head, but even so, I recognised him straight away. When he raised a hand to scratch at the hairs there, I realised he was wearing a wedding ring. For some reason I found myself smiling. It certainly seemed a day for coincidences. I left my seat so that I could go to the toilet, but really so that I could check on him when I returned.

Whilst I was in the tiny cubicle the train pulled into Ely Station. There is always a sense of disorientation when the train leaves Ely, as it returns some way back down the track it has come along before veering off in a new direction. When I'd seen Melanie that morning, we'd actually had to swap seats again at Ely so that she could continue to face the direction we were travelling. By that time we were already well acquainted, and she'd pushed her body past mine to get to her seat. That, in a way, had sealed the undercurrent of conversation which had passed between us.

But in the toilet the sensation of leaving and returning within moments made me feel faint. Instead of standing to pee, I sat down on the seat. Beads of sweat prickled my forehead, and for a moment I held my face in my hands. I thought of Emma, and how she must never know what I'd done. Pulling Melanie's phone number out of my pocket, I tore the pieces of paper into strips, and then flushed them down the toilet. Even so, I couldn't get rid of the feeling of completeness I had felt when I was with her. I shook my head, and returned to the carriage.

As I passed Dermot's seat, I saw it was now empty. Not only that, but someone was sitting where I had been. Presumably Dermot had left at Ely, and someone else had boarded to take my seat. I glanced up at my briefcase in the overhead rack and seeing that it was still there I decided to take Dermot's seat for the rest of the journey. It was easier than making a fuss. What did it matter where I sat anyway?

The train passed through Thetford and then Attleborough. I found myself losing the sickly feeling and regaining the ability to think rationally. Maybe it was because of its transient nature, but I found that my memories of the sex with Melanie were already fading. If I really thought about it, I could almost convince myself that nothing had happened. That was certainly the state of mind in which I would have to greet Emma when I got home. Destroying Melanie's number made it all the less tangible. Perhaps we genuinely hadn't fucked at all.

Remembering my glimpse of Dermot, I took a look at the wedding ring on my own hand.

It wasn't there.

I stared at the impression of a ring on my finger, but even as I looked the indentation seemed to close over, as though I'd never worn a ring at all. I shook my head, rubbed my eyes; all the usual things that one is supposed to do to restore reality. But when I looked again there was no change. Panic rose up in my throat. This was hardly something I could hide from Emma. I tried to remember if I'd taken the ring off when checking into the hotel. Maybe I'd done so subconsciously, diverting any feelings of guilt. But if so, it certainly wasn't in any of my pockets now.

I remembered Melanie then, pulling at my fingers as she led me to bed, a smile on her face that promised all that I eventually took. Had she somehow slipped off my ring in that moment? I thought of the piece of paper with her phone number on it, torn, sodden, and blown all over the Ely tracks.

I decided against telling Emma I'd been robbed. It was too complicated, didn't make any sense. I'd only trip myself up over the details. Instead I'd say I took off the ring when washing in the conference centre, that I was trying to remove the traces of thick black marker pen that had stained my hands during the presentation. This wasn't entirely untrue, and as I thought through the idea faint marks appeared on my hands accordingly. The story sounded stupid enough to be believable. I'd pretend to make some calls to the centre to see if anyone had handed in a missing ring. I'd blame a rush to the train, anything, for leaving it on the edge of the sink. I toyed with the idea of saying it fell into the plughole, but dismissed the idea. She'd want to know why I hadn't called a plumber or someone to retrieve it. Besides, intimating knowledge of its whereabouts felt wrong.

As the train pulled into Norwich I got up ready to leave. I felt redeemed. There was always a crush as the train pulled into the station at this time of day. People just wanted to get home.

Ahead of me, close to the door, I saw the top of Dermot's head through the crowd.

As we left the train I struggled to keep up with him. He kept flipping out of sight, like a smaller fish swimming with larger fish. Weaving in and out, disappearing and reappearing, blinking on and off. Just as I remembered him.

In the car park I saw him enter a Volvo similar to mine. Then I realised my car was still at the garage, so I headed for the taxi rank. In my haste I was first in the queue, and I pretended to the driver that I didn't know the address although I knew the way there. Without him realising, we started to follow Dermot.

My mobile beeped a new message as we turned down Riverside Road, but I didn't want any distractions so I ignored it. To my left the river ran alongside us in the opposite direction. I was reminded of Ely Station, and the view of the cathedral over the river on our approach which was then reversed on our return. I remembered sitting on a sofa at a party, then standing in a corner. I remembered a kick in the face, and then a kick in the balls. When Dermot's car turned right at the roundabout and headed up Kett's Hill towards

Plumstead Road, I knew he was going to my house and I knew all that I had lost and all that I had gained.

My phone beeped again. A reminder.

Dermot pulled into my drive and the taxi kept going. I thought I could see Emma's reflection behind the glass in the kitchen, but then she became no more than a memory. I didn't tell him to stop, but after a while the taxi pulled over, the driver leaning over the front seats to talk to me.

"Listen mate, I don't mind following other cars around but as we've left him behind, do you mind telling me where we're going?"

I flipped open my mobile and read Melanie's message:
'One moment you're in the right group, then you're in the wrong group'.

I'd have to text her to ask her where we lived.

# ANDREW HOOK

Frustrated with the ever-shrinking market for short stories, Norwich resident **Andrew Hook** took the brave (some might say foolhardy) decision to set up his own publishing business: 'Elastic Press'. Already an established author in the independent press and elsewhere, Andrew launched the imprint with a collection of his own work, *The Virtual Menagerie*, in 2002. The book made an immediate impression by being shortlisted for a British Fantasy Award in 2003.

Elastic Press have since gone from strength to strength, quickly gaining a reputation for innovative projects – the 2006 anthology *Extended Play* features stories by authors inspired by music and essays by musicians (including members of Blondie, Snow Patrol and the Stranglers) on how their music has been influenced by stories – and Tony Richards' *Going Back* (May 2007) marks their twenty-second publication in a little under five years. Various collections and individual stories have been in the running for awards along the way, with Elastic Press themselves winning the 'Best Small Press' category in the 2005 British Fantasy Awards.

Andrew now has more than sixty published short stories to his credit in a variety of different genres. His second slipstream collection, *Beyond Each Blue Horizon*, appeared in 2005, and a collection of mainstream stories, *Residue,* was published in 2006. Nor does he restrict himself to short fiction, with his debut novel, *Moon Beaver*, being published by ENC Press in 2004 and a second novel completed, for which he is currently seeking a publisher.

# ADAM ROBERTS

**Adam Roberts** was born two-thirds of the way through the twentieth century. He now lives a little way west of London with his wife and daughter, and works teaching English and Creative Writing at Royal Holloway, University of London. He has several academic publications to his credit – many of them on the subject of nineteenth-century literature – and eight novels to date, most recently *Land of the Headless* (Gollancz 2007) and *Splinter* (Solaris 2007), as well as a fair deal of shorter fiction. Two of his novels, *Salt* (Gollancz 2000) and *Gradisil* (Gollancz 2006), have been shortlisted for the prestigious Arthur C. Clarke Award.

Of 'Remorse' he says: 'The title *disLOCATIONS* suggested to me, at first, a landscape, a place-out-of-joint; but when I thought about it further I found myself wondering about the emotional landscapes that shape our lives so much more than physical ones; the intensities like high places, the depressions like fog-filled valleys. *Then* I thought to myself how widespread is the desire that, in punishing malefactors, we could make them feel the evil that they have done: we all want not just to hurt or imprison their external bodies, we want to reach their souls, the centres of their remorse. The story is about the emotional dislocations that might follow the creation of a drug that achieves precisely that aim.'

# REMORSE®

by
## Adam Roberts

It's on.

Yep. Hep. Yeah.

So, this is my understanding of how we came to be here. And the least I can do to give you my sense of how we got here, how we arrived as it were. It happened like this. Remorse® was developed by the Pharmakon Corporation, using a smile-shaped wedge of governmental money, on account of drug development being so billions-expensive. It was initially designed as a treatment for certain psychopathologies in which individuals who lacked human empathic skills could be given the help they needed. It's a – I've seen it – I mean I've seen it in its medical format – it's a museum-piece now, of course – it was a lozenge, a small pellet, like a Go pebble. White one, black one. And you placed this under the tongue, I think. Which is to say, no, I'm getting this wrong. I'm sorry! It wasn't under the tongue, of course not. Sorry! Sorry! It was a lozenge, but you pressed it up against the roof of your mouth, and the nanofoam got itself going, set its pathways tentacling, and insinuated its way into the brain pan. Sorry!

Okay. So. Imagine a sociopath. They tested it on psychopaths and murderers first of all, you see. Not that there's a centre in the brain where remorse is, you know, generated. I'm sorry if I gave you that impression, I really am, that would be misleading. Killer kills because he is untroubled about the violence he inflicts on others. Killer kills because it makes him feel powerful and immune, and that power and that immunity depend upon the thing-ness of the victim. You cut a throat, and it's only a throat, not a whole living, terrified human being. It's not even a throat. It's just a mechanism by which the killer reinforces his superhumanity. Or so

77

I understand it to have been. Obviously – I want to be clear about this. I don't want to give you a false impression – obviously I really don't understand the motivation of such people. I'm sure you don't either. But we can both agree that they need treatment.

So Remorse® becomes a treatment for crime, all of it, crime as a whole. Put it in the water! That was the famous slogan, the famous slogan the Blanchett slogan! And why not put it in the water supply? Not for nothing was it called the utopia drug by, I'm sorry, I'm sorry I can't remember who said that. But it was a well chosen word, don't you think?

A dilution, a development of the pharmochemistry: dose up certain populations, that's the idea. Because if we give Hannibal Lecter this pill, we discover that he empathises too much with his victim to kill them. He can't do it any more. His victim is no longer a thing, his victim is a person. Just pulling the knife from its sheath maketh the killer for to burst into tears, to throw himself on the floor 'I'm sorry! I'm sorry!' And if it works, in large dose, for such extreme criminals, then might it not, in smaller doses, might it not take the edge off the whole crime wave? Damp down the tsunami? Could you steal someone's car if your mental threshold for remorse were raised, just a little? Could you mug someone if you empathised fully with the victim? Of course not.

I'll tell you something else, too: it was – I remember this – I'm sorry, I'm a bit disjointed in my narrative here. I'm sorry! It must be somehow annoying for you to have to listen to this rambling – this rambling. Look: I remember how it was, and I remember one of the reasons there was such widespread support for the drug. (Put it in the water!) Let's say you arrest Hannibal Lecter. Let's say you punish him. He's grinning the whole time. You put him in prison – do what you like, starve him, beat him, make him lie on a wet mattress (oh God just to think of it!) and pass electric current through it – and he's grinning at you. You see, you can't touch the core of his evil mind. You want to, but you can't. You don't want just to hurt his body. You want him to feel the pain he has inflicted. You want to take the pain he has created and inject it into his mind.

Now you can. The drug made that possible. It's a boon to justice.

And it does reduce crime levels. It does guard against terrorism. And it does preserve the peace, and does all that simply by raising the natural human response to the pain of others. Even to contemplate a crime can cause overwhelming gushing levels of remorse to flood the mind. I know, as you know, because we all know, now that it's in the water.

Mr Blanchett? Too tight? OK, I'm sorry, OK, I'm sorry. Sorry, there, there, there.

Now, things were of course better, things were, and it's a simple move to 'expand the definition' of crime to include political malefaction. So people don't rape and rob any more because even so much as planning the crime brings on agonizing bouts of remorse. So it's not hard to refine the drug, such that planning to overthrow the government as a terrorist might, and planning to vote-out the government as a voter might, become pretty much the same thing. Opposing the government brings with it prolonged and agonizing bouts of remorse. And I vote – I voted at the last election, and with a clear conscience, and for your administration too! Isn't the world better now? I remember how it was before, when you couldn't walk from house to store without risking gunjacking. Much better now. And I've often wondered if there's a connection between the remorse response in the brain and the gratitude response. I'm grateful, certainly. I'm grateful for what the drug has done to society.

Of course, the, what you might call... I'm sorry, what you might call side-effects. There are side-effects. A lot of people are timid. Some are pretty cowed, I guess. Some take it bad, can barely leave their homes for fear of – you know – of whatever they might, accidentally or intentionally – you know. But others function pretty well. And then there are those who... well, take me. Here's the example of me.

I did try, for a time, to pick a path so as to avoid feeling this ramped-up remorse. I attempted, and this is not a figure of speech, not to hurt a fly. But then I came to an understanding. I call it self-revelation. Remorse is an intensity. It is an extreme focus of self-awareness and other-awareness. It's – in a word – look, I'm sorry to use this word, but it's sex. And, no, that's not good enough, for it's more intense than sex, provided only. Look: here's what I mean.

79

This stiletto, it's better than a cock. The point on your skin, it's –
it's – there's an exquisite. There's a, and the force, the pressure of
muscles that –

I'm sorry!
I'm sorry!
I'm sorry!
I'm sorry!
I'm sorry!
I'm sorry!
I'm sorry!
Aaaaaaa.

I always do that, say it seven times I mean. I don't plan to, it
just comes out that way, as knife goes in. As blood comes out. Ah,
the ecstasy of it. The sevenfold ecstasy of it! And, yes, it's true I
come, yes it's true my heart goes poppity-pupoppity, but it's not
just – sorry – here, let me loosen that a little – there you go. Sorry
the floor's bare concrete, Senator, but I'll need to clean it shortly,
and carpet would be – well, you can imagine. But, Senator, what I
was saying, what I was saying, is that although my body makes
manifest certain symptoms of physical desire, the… not that I don't
prepare for that. I'm wearing plastic boxers, for instance: I learnt
that lesson right at the start, after the very first of them! But the
intensity with which my excitement and my agony at your pain is
mixed together, that's more than just a physical thing. That's a
transcendent feeling. That's religious. It unites me with you, and
with the cosmos, as with – aaaaa.

There you go, and goodbye Senator. I'm really sorry. Really
sorry, really I am. Thanks for all you've done! It's made the world
of difference to me. It's put me in touch with – well. Humanity. It
has.

# THE CONVENTION

by
Amanda Hemingway

They advertised it as Fantasy New York: the Convention, generally abbreviated to FanNYcon. It was one of the most important events in the fantasy calendar, attracting publishers, publicists, authors, aspiring authors, would-be aspiring authors, bottom-drawer novelists, fans, geeks, freaks, and herds of nerds. Despite this, hotels had competed for the business, knowing all of the attendees would drink expensively and long.

Merlin Stone arrived from London on the second day in order to look cool, although it was his first major convention and he was a guest, ranked just below a minor vampire from Buffy, an actor who had had one line in the original Star Wars, and a horse from Lord of the Rings. His Foulweather trilogy had enjoyed huge success in the States, with raves in the likes of Santa Cruz News and the Baltimore Literary Review, he had been nominated for the Fibula and shortlisted for the Sago, and was credited with single-handedly influencing the attitude of Middle America to global warming, though no one was sure in what way.

His sword-and-sorcery epic was set in a post-apocalyptic world of blasted landscapes and dubious meteorology, populated by subhuman goblins (dorcs) and ruled by a gang of pseudo-mediaeval Hell's Angels. Their leader, Skanc, had found the infamous Torc of Everdark, but didn't know how to wield it, and wanted to capture Erik, the Child of Prophecy, and force him to help. But Erik had come under the protection of Rorc, the martial-arts champion and anti-hero, former Dragonsword of Quaik and Firespear of Ultimate Dawn, now part-time tomb-raider and disillusioned mercenary. Pursued by sinister Hoodies (hooded riders mounted on giant blood-sucking sheep, called rampyres) and aided by the elvish supermodel Neowyn, they had to defeat Skanc and his ally, the voluptuous enchantress Mortittia, destroy the Torc, and stop a vast tsunami from engulfing the Greenvale where the few remaining good-but-helpless peasants were in retreat. Merlin (real name Douglas Niggle), who was thirty-five but admitted to sixteen, had mastered quickly the essential constituents of the genre: gory battle-scenes, turgid description, imaginative torture and unimaginative sex, and was now hailed as the greatest thing in a direct line of greatest things (Robert Jordan, Stephen Donaldson etc) since Tolkien.

Enthusiastic publishers had actually offered to buy him dinner, should he attend the convention, and had booked him a room on the fiftieth floor of the Megatron-Marplush hotel where it was being held. (Unfortunately, the fiftieth floor wasn't built yet, and he ended up sleeping in someone else's room on the forty-first.)

Arriving at the hotel, Merlin found himself engulfed in a crowd of orcs in spiky armour, barbarian warriors in spiky armour with horns, amazons in spiky armour with breastplates, Ringwraiths (black cloak and hood), Siths (black cloak and hood) and Jedi (black cloak and hood). He mistook several of them for characters in his own books, and was deeply gratified. Calling the publicist, Kelly Blumenglum, on her cellphone, he found she was at a film party too exclusive for him to attend, but he had a programme of signings and panels for the next two days and they would surely meet up soon. Following instructions, Merlin made his way to the publisher's booth on the Lower Ground where he was greeted with bright smiles, a stack of books to sign, and a queue of three. At an adjacent table, a female writer in a drooping skirt, a top with drooping sleeves, and a drooping bosom, was holding up an apparently endless line of fans while she demanded a cushion for her elbow. Merlin was told she was Sorrel J. Cameltown, a bestseller producing elvish erotica thinly disguised as alternate reality chick lit. "My right arm is completely exhausted," she complained in a fragile voice.

'I'll bet it is,' Merlin found himself thinking nastily. (Who was it who said: 'The problem with writers is that they have too much time to masturbate'?) Then he decided, with a twinge of guilt, that this was not in keeping with the convention spirit – whatever that was – and settled down to his own signing.

By evening he had done two debating panels – The Prevalence of Jungian Thought in Twentieth Century Fantasy and Sex and the Single Orc – and wandered in a state of schoolboy bliss round the Sales section, spending his credit card on things he didn't need and would probably never be allowed to take on the plane. There was enough assorted weaponry to arm a small revolution, rails of spandex bodywear, cuddly demons and embroidered shoulder dragons, plastic and ceramic models of everyone from Gandalf and Belgarath to Morthbild the Unbreastable, T-shirts printed with Beam me up Scotty, May the Force be with you, and the rather more ambiguous Love me love my Preciouss. You could buy a Darth Vader helmet complete with voice box, an inflatable Lucy Lawless, the pectorals of Conan the Barbarian, the sideburns of Wolverine, the bananas of Bananaman. Grown men relapsed into adolescence as they piled up the purchases, ostensibly for their children – "Do you think a triple-bladed kriss is really suitable for little Wayne, darling?" – or, in the case of true nerds, to add to collections of same. When Merlin finally dragged himself away, unsure what to do next and feeling vaguely hungry, he fell in with a kindly couple from one of the panels who took him to the bar.

"We're veterans of these events," the woman explained. She had violet hair and a motley of multi-coloured clothes and looked like a motherly witch. "Of course I'm not a big star like you, but I've published two short stories, one of which came fifth in the Enterprose Awards, and Harvey here has been working on a film script for the last ten years. George Lucas is really interested."

It's very nice to be called a big star, especially when you aren't. Merlin bought a round of drinks.

The woman, whose name appeared to be Minerva ('Call me Min'), studied a programme in order to discuss party options for the evening. At the top of the list was the All-the-Terrys party, for writers called Terry, and the launch of the latest Gerald R.R.R.R. Morton, the seventh tome in his new trilogy, where each book was longer than the last, and the end receded further and further away the more you read. Then there was yet another promotion for the widely publicised Da Winky Code, a piece of fictionalised faction which claimed the Harry Potter books had actually been written by an Oriental monk in the fifteenth century, Rau Ling, concealed by his house elf, and passed down through the years via a secret conspiracy of fantasy writers and artists. Clues included the significance of the H.P. in H.P. Lovecraft, a Freudian misprint in a Wagner libretto, producing the title Pötterdämmerung, a pair of spectacles drawn on a Botticelli Cupid by the painter himself, and the hidden word Muggle in the name of The Smuggler's Rest, a West Country pub once frequented by Michael Moorcock.

"I haven't read it," Merlin confessed.

"Oh, but you must," said Min, shocked. "I mean, I know it's fiction but there must be truth in it somewhere, mustn't there? Otherwise the Catholic church wouldn't have tried to suppress it."

"Did they?"

"Of course," Harvey said. "Witchcraft, you know. And," he dropped his voice several tones, perhaps because someone dressed as a cardinal had seated himself at a nearby table, "you must have heard of Opus Magnum."

"What's Opus Magnum?"

"A secret organisation of suicide priests trained in martial arts. They wear bondage kit under their black robes, whip each other twice a day, and, worst of all, they are compelled to grow moustaches."

"How awful," said Merlin, who couldn't think of anything else to say. "But they don't sound very secret to me. You know about them, after all. And black robes would rather stand out in a crowd."

"Except," said Harvey with a wealth of hidden meaning, "at a fantasy convention..." He was obviously partial to speaking in italics.

Merlin digested these ominous undercurrents while Min canvassed the lower echelons of the party list. This consisted mostly of parties thrown – or at least dropped – by the kind of countries which, despairing of film festivals and other international events, thought it would be cool to host fantasy conventions instead, and so put in an appearance in the hope of attracting business. These included places like Lithuania, Moldova, Outer Mongolia, Kirgizstan, and anywhere in Scandinavia. "Anybody can go to those parties," Harvey explained. "You don't need an invitation. And there's free drink."

"Any food?" Merlin asked. His hunger pangs were scarcely alleviated by the bowl of peanuts on the table.

"In a way," said Harvey.

Encouraged by Min, Merlin phoned Kelly Blumenglum yet again. Although she was unfortunately too busy to meet with him, she declared she had left his invitation to the incredibly exclusive Da Winky party on reception. When Merlin located it, accompanied by his escort, he found it marked Special and Personal and Admit One Only, but the other two seemed undeterred. "We'll all go," they assured him happily, and hustled him off to a couple of lesser parties by way of a warm-up.

At a do hosted by Lapland, they had minced reindeer balls and snowpunch, which seemed to be white wine diluted with industrial vodka. This compared favourably with the Chatø Strømsø served by Sweden, with open sandwiches of cured dragonbreast (smaugasbord). Outer Mongolia offered fermented mare's milk (high on milk, low on ferment) and corn chips made of fried yurt. The best food – and, to Merlin's surprise, the best booze – were supplied by Oman, though no one was quite sure what they were doing there. "Oil money," Harvey opined darkly. Most of his opinions were dark. "They probably think they're at a convention on international terrorism."

"I don't think Oman has much of that," Merlin said.

"Exactly," Harvey said triumphantly. "They're here to learn."

With all the weaponry in the Sales hall, Merlin reflected, they wouldn't find it difficult.

"What are these gorgeous crispy round things?" he asked by way of a change of subject.

"Battered sheep's eyes," Harvey said, knowledgeably. Like most people with dark opinions, he was given to being extremely knowledgeable about any subject, even when he didn't actually know very much about it.

Merlin set down his plate and thought wistfully of hamburgers – this was America, wasn't it? But when he suggested going to eat, Harvey and Min swept such trivia aside.

"Time for the big one," they said, and carried him along to the Liberace Ballroom for the Da Winky party.

Bouncers in tuxedos scanned his invitation suspiciously. "Are you on the list?" they asked. Merlin had no idea, but gave his name, and was duly approved. "What about them?"

"We're his entourage," said Min.

"Bodyguards," said Harvey. "He's wanted by Opus Magnum."

Several black-robed figures nearby glanced their way, but Merlin wasn't paying attention. The party looked rather enticing, with tall glasses of what appeared to be champagne, vast trays of canapés, and groups of guests in exotic costumes deep in what was surely serious literary conversation. Suddenly, the crowd parted, and he saw a girl – a girl such as he had only dreamed of or written about, a girl with comic-strip curves in some kind of scarlet clingfilm, gold thigh-boots with five-inch heels, a mane of chestnut hair, a huge sultry pout. A girl a million lightyears away from the motherly Minerva. He moved forward to glide through the party into her arms...

"You're not on the list," a bouncer was saying to Harvey and Min. "Sorry. No entry."

Merlin couldn't help feeling very slightly relieved. A break from his new friends would be welcome. "See you later," he said, veering back to the girl as a compass needle towards magnetic north.

"Oh, but you can't go without us," Min said, seizing his arm in a vice-like grip. "We've bonded."

"If we can't all go, then no one will go," Harvey declared in the accents of union solidarity, as if he were the one rejecting the party.

"But – but –" stammered Merlin. It was no good. Min's armlock would indeed have qualified her as a bodyguard, had she so desired. Harvey, though lacking her Schwarzenegger muscle-tone, clearly made up for it with Jedi mind-powers.

"We're your friends," he reminded Merlin. "Friends stick together. All for one and one for all. It looked like a crap party, anyway. You wouldn't want to go."

"I wouldn't want to go," echoed Merlin, mesmerised.

"That isn't real champagne, you know. Just the cheap stuff. You'd be bored out of your mind."

"Bored out of my mind," said Merlin dully.

"We'll go back to the bar," Harvey dictated.

"Back to the bar..."

They went back to the bar.

Merlin mumbled something about hamburgers, but Harvey and Min were set on joining other party rejects over endless glasses of thin American beer, urine-coloured and chilled out of all flavour. Merlin felt the sort of depressing sobriety setting in which no amount of drink can cure.

The peanuts had run out.

Later that same century, the aftermath of the party arrived, sparkling with champagne and trailing glamour, their costumes rumpled as if with the fervour of their revels. Merlin wanted to perk up, but decided it was too late. A black-robed figure sidled up to him, exuding bewilderment and a sinister foreign accent. "Is thees the convention on eenternational terroreesm?"

"Oh no," said a man Merlin thought he recognised as a well-known SF writer. "You want the Glitz, on Central Park."

"Thank you," murmured the black robe with a slight bow, and hurried out.

Other black robes remained, ordering drinks and patting concealed moustaches.

And there was the girl, looking more improbably gorgeous than ever, the scarlet latex (or whatever it was) clinging to her smooth shapely limbs without a crease, the gold thigh-boots clinging to her long shapely legs, her whole image one of general clingingness and shapeliness guaranteed to reduce Merlin's very thought processes to gibbering idiocy. Arriving at the party, he had felt confident and successful, a genuine guest with a genuine invitation – a writer among writers – at least until Min dragged him away. But now, in his current state of sober gloom, he realised that such a girl would never have a word to say to him. He was dull and boring, surrounded by losers, too pathetic or too polite to shake them off. He saw her turn to the SF writer, who was not just famous but also unfairly attractive, and resigned himself to a long night suffering the pangs of unrequited lust.

He had risen to his feet with the arrival of the ex-partygoers and suddenly he felt himself grabbed in an armlock for the second time – bloody Min, he thought, and fury and frustration took over.

He drove his elbow backwards in a vicious jab and heard his assailant grunt in agony. He spun round in dawning horror... but it wasn't Min. The figure doubled up behind him wore a black robe and seemed to have dropped his moustache.

"What the hell —"

"Brother Tim!" said a fellow black robe. "Are you okay?" And to Merlin: "How dare you?"

"He attacked me!"

"Of course he didn't! He was just —"

'Wanted,' wheezed Brother Tim, who, beneath the disguise of hood and moustache, seemed to be a small nondescript person looking rather like a tortoise out of its shell. "The organisation... want... He's one of them."

"No I'm not!" Merlin protested indignantly. No one wants to be described as one of them, even if he has no idea who they are.

"We'll get him," said the other black robe, who was considerably taller and bulkier than Brother Tim. "Long live Saint Thomas of Magnum!"

"You'll have to get past us first," said Minerva. For once, Merlin was glad of her Terminator muscletone.

The commotion had drawn the attention of several ex-partygoers, including The Girl. "Are you really wanted by Opus Magnum?" she asked Merlin.

"Well..." he temporised.

"That's so exciting," she persisted. The SF writer had clearly been outclassed. "Aren't you scared? I mean, they've got members everywhere. They've totally infiltrated this convention. Look around you."

There were, indeed, a number of black robes in the bar, drinking under their hoods.

"I can handle it," Merlin said, nonchalantly. He'd done that kind of nonchalance on paper so often he found it was quite easy in real life. Also he knew perfectly well he wasn't wanted by anybody, except his creditors.

Brother Tim and his colleague had got into a row with Harvey and Min which seemed to be keeping all concerned happily preoccupied, and Merlin felt able to give all his attention to the girl. It wasn't difficult.

"I love your outfit," he said. 'Are you supposed to be someone?' And then, realising that was badly phrased: "Like – like a book character or something."

"Oh no," she said. "I always dress like this."

"R-really?"

"For conventions. I go to lots. It's my job."

"Are you – are you a writer?" Merlin stammered. She didn't look at all like a writer.

"Publicity," the girl explained. "My name's Kelly."

"Not – Kelly Blumenglum?" Kelly who had already brushed him off twice. Could he somehow avoid telling her who he was?

Evidently not.

"That's right. Who're you? We can't have met – I'd have remembered."

"Actually, I'm Merlin. Merlin Stone. We've spoken on your cell…"

"Oh my God!" She gave a peal of laughter, showing perfect teeth. Or at least, perfectly capped. 'What an amazing coincidence. But why didn't you tell me everything? If I'd known you were wanted by Opus Magnum I'd have included it in your promo. I mean, that really ups your profile here. I must get you some more interviews. And there's a party tomorrow for the new fantasy novel by that crazy British senator – George Something – it's just so exclusive, everybody will be there. I'll get you an invite. Apparently the book's about this heroic dictator who defies an evil superpower with some magical secret weapons… I think it's for the kids' market. Of course, it hasn't been written yet but they're starting the publicity right now to get the ball rolling. But why weren't you at the Da Winky party? I left your invite on reception.'

Merlin opened his mouth to explain, but didn't get the chance.

"How stupid of me – of course you couldn't go – Opus Magnum were there in force. I must say, I think it's amazingly brave of you to be here at all. Can I get you a cocktail or something? It's all on expenses."

"Actually," Merlin said, emboldened, "I'm starving. I'd really like a hamburger."

"Great. We'll go out. I know this fantastic place – open all night. Can you meet me in the lobby? I need the bathroom."

Just in time Merlin, who had mastered cell but not bathroom, realised he was up against the language barrier and she wasn't expecting to take a shower break. He said: "Fine," and followed more slowly as she left the bar.

On the way, he passed Harvey and Min, now discussing the new Dr Who with their erstwhile enemies. Wrapped in a warm glow which included an unexpected element of gratitude, Merlin stopped to say goodnight and even expressed a desire to meet tomorrow.

"Are those guys really in Opus Magnum?" he asked Harvey in an aside.

"Oh no," Harvey said, rather less darkly than usual. "They're from a retirement complex in Tallahassee. But heck, this is FanNYcon. You can be what you like."

"Good," said Merlin, now thoroughly in the mood. He thought of Kelly Blumenglum, and decided he was going to be a very successful writer, a superhero, and possibly an Olympic lover. Just for tonight.

After all, that's fantasy.

# AMANDA HEMINGWAY

**Amanda Hemingway** is confident that she has been both born and (partially) educated, although she remains a little hazy as to the details. She *is* aware that she knows too little about string theory, cosmic expansion, possible cures for cancer, ancient Aztec poetry and many areas of contemporary fiction – not to mention darning socks and making pastry. Before settling on her current occupation as a writer, Amanda travelled the world and supported herself through a variety of professions, including that of actress, barmaid, garage hand, laboratory assistant, journalist, and model.

Amanda made her speculative fiction debut in *Introduction 7* (1981), with the occult novella "The Alchemist", followed a year later by her debut novel *Psyche* – a highly original SF tale which won the 'Most Promising First Novel Award' from the Southeastern Arts Association. Four more novels followed before Amanda reinvented herself in the new millennium, emerging as **Jan Siegel**, under which name she released the successful *Prospero's Children* (2001) and two further 'Fern Capel' novels. Despite reverting to her own name for the critically acclaimed *Sangreal Trilogy*, which began with *The Greenstone Grail* (Voyager, 2005), Amanda has continued to toy with multiple identities, releasing two romantic comedy 'chic lit' novels under the name **Jemma Harvey** during the same period.

Amanda is presently working on a new fantasy novel, the first of a projected series, whilst concurrently writing a story for younger children. The latter is something of a departure for her. Goodness only knows what name *that* book might appear under!

# ANDY WEST

Having originally trained in physics, **Andy West** has subsequently pursued a career in software and product management. A long-time SF fan and a member of the Northampton SF Writers Group, Andy also has a passionate interest in the mechanisms of history and the underlying evolutionary constraints on societies, which frequently manifests in his writing. His stories tend to place the mathematics of life firmly centre-stage. Andy's first published piece, the novella "Meme", appeared in serialised form across four issues of the webzine *Bewildering Stories*, and featured in that publication's 'best of' edition for the first quarter of 2007.

"Impasse" takes place in a vividly realised future where humanity has diverged into varied forms. As well as highlighting an individual's struggle against mortality, the story also explores the evolutionary purpose and boundaries of death. It is set in the same universe as *The Clonir Flower*, an epic novel for which Andy is actively seeking a publisher. He is currently hard at work on a collaborative project with celebrated author Ian Watson – a techno-thriller, which represents an exciting departure for both of them.

Andy recently moved to Stony Stratford, which boasts two neighbouring pubs, 'The Cock' and 'The Bull', said to have given rise to a particular brand of storytelling. Despite enjoying the hospitality of both these establishments, Andy insists they have not as yet influenced his own writing to any noticeable degree.

# IMPASSE

by
Andy West

*Mortality mortality,
evolution's reality.*

Swift Might blundered through mires of black sludge and castellated wastes of umber crystal. He shattered impeding formations of ancient minerals with prodigious fists or great gouts of fire. His course ploughed the surface as straight as a furrow, but in truth he was going nowhere. Occasionally he paused to hurl fury and frustration at the indifferent stars.

No matter how fast his progress, harrowing nightmares still trailed the edge of his awareness: bitter betrayal embodied in the guise of Steel Rage, the astonishing ferocity of Eye of Storm's attack, the ignominy of defeat and flight, the wreck of his fatally damaged craft. Behind all these and other torturing visions lurked the ultimate nightmare. Its scarcely acknowledged names pushed their way into his consciousness; The Nothing, The Dissolution, the greatest failure of all.

Swift Might redoubled his pace. He, who had always taken whatever he wanted and scorned the hope of inferiors, now chased that tiny light to the limit of his strength. Though the odds were against it, he assured himself that somewhere on this forlorn rock there had to be a prospecting team or a raider's lair, maybe an automated processing plant or a navigation beacon; anything that would enable him to claw his way back to civilisation and plot his revenge.

Pain was Swift Might's constant companion. Not just from his ragged wounds. He'd tried to isolate the nerve circuits around those, though needling messages of hurt still found their way through. But there was no possible isolation from the aching confusion that riddled his ageing mind. In addition to swelling rates of error, the many extensions and peripheral upgrades, greedily acquired to maintain supremacy, threatened to submerge his faltering core.

Sorely injured and robbed of his high status among the Au-Sek, the great burden of creeping dysfunction was much harder to bear and more difficult to control. Although Swift Might refused to acknowledge the fact, the speed of his action was dulled and his might was no longer so mighty.

His concentration wandered and his urgent scanning of the desolate horizon at all frequencies lapsed. The loss of his fortress home on Ceres sapped him like a physical blow. Standantima, 'Stands against time', had been the looming symbol of his dominance. Its soaring blue-black battlements, sibilating shields and massive armament demanded the greatest respect. Traders and raiders from the highest of the alien Worlds had humbled themselves before him, earning mercy or hard judgement at his whim.

Irony gripped Swift Might. Standantima still held back the march of time, but no longer from him. No doubt Eye of Storm ruled there now, while The Dissolution pursued a once-feared chief across this puny asteroid.

His anger was the only force keeping him going. He contemplated the balm of revenge. But spells of dizziness swept across him like violent gusts of wind, bringing a more impenetrable blackness than the spangled dark of space.

Then he was on his hands and knees. He didn't recall how. His palms pressed against something smooth and flat. He gazed downwards. A glimmer of reflected starlight met his eye. He released some Sonics and a little Ultra-Violet, overlaying their returned waves: methane ice. His perception descended into a pearly domain of refracting planes and scintillating crystals. This entire universe of interacting geometry was utterly at rest. Yet a cold, opaque heart seemed to shift, beckoning....

Swift Might abruptly cut off his signals. Pale vapour had enwrapped his arms. He recoiled, then rose and hurriedly restarted his trek. He chided himself. Above all he had to maintain discipline! Why did those bizarre tales from the primordial people of Earth, so amusing back on Ceres, have to creep up on him now? There were no wraiths beyond The Dissolution. Such a notion was ridiculous. Beyond was just endless nothing, and to fall into that pool of absence was heinous failure.

Yet only minutes later he was falling. He recovered from another lapse in concentration, just too late to avoid breaking through a crumbling ledge. His instinctively outstretched senses revealed a wide ravine and a considerable drop, though this wasn't a concern in itself. Gravity was too light for a harmful impact. But metallic objects on the floor below triggered a spark of hope, which was quickly doused by a flood of fear.

Swift Might landed flat on his back, yet with a true warrior's reflex he rolled and leapt up in a split second, shoulder weapons blazing and fists swinging. If his opponents were surprised, they didn't show it. With impressive speed four Aumons ducked his fire and sprang at him as one. His chop crushed the chest of the first before the other three were upon him. He was ignominiously felled, unable to bring limbs or weapons to bear. He bucked and heaved, but acting like a single entity the remaining Aumons formed an efficient net that clung ever tighter, pinning him fast to the ground.

It was physical impasse! Swift Might could not fight, could barely even move. But the much slighter, skeletal Aumons were fully occupied with holding him down. They couldn't spare a single appendage with which to inflict damage. Further, they were unarmed while he was extremely robust in his articulated shell of practically impenetrable plate alloy.

All motion ceased. Yet the conflict continued, rolling into another domain.

Swift Might had never actually encountered Aumons before. But he knew that despite a wholly alien culture and radically different modes of survival, the essential substance of their being was much like his own. The physique he considered puny was nevertheless constructed around a core of steel and carbon-fibre, like some diminutive designer's model of the grand Au-Sek frame he occupied. Aumon thoughts, which he considered disgustingly communal and timid, nevertheless flew on photons and electrons just as his did. The creatures that bound him were electroptic forms, sharing a common ancestry with his own Race.

Swift Might's memory did not contain trivial data regarding when the Au-Sek line had split from its Aumonic roots, but it did contain data about vulnerable electromagnetic windows into Aumon thought. He transmitted withering blasts in the high microwave region, carefully monitoring the mental activity of his clinging adversaries between each pulse.

The Aumons twitched and trembled, clearly suffering, but their grip remained tight. The whispering signatures of their thought stumbled, but did not stop. With mounting frustration Swift Might poured out different wavelengths and pulse-widths, battering the mental walls of his enemy and probing mercilessly for a weak spot. He also managed to twist his head and aim screaming Sonics into the unprotected face of the nearest Aumon.

Swift Might felt victory was within his grasp. Confidently, he stretched his capabilities to the utmost, increasing still further the intensity of his assault. These lowly workers must have a ship. As the hope of escape shone through his core, the darkness of The Dissolution receded.

Then cold intrusion buffeted his thoughts of triumph. Strange images engulfed him. His concentration blundered about, not going where he knew it should. Realisation struck Swift Might hard. The inferior Aumons had somehow crept inside him. They were trying to hi-jack his mind!

A jolt of dread helped him resist and cling to awareness and identity. This prompted a flash of insight too; he realised the Aumons were winning because they acted as one entity. He did not truly face three feeble Aumons, but a single sentience of much greater capability. He had to break this formidable opponent into manageable pieces!

Swift Might trawled through millions of empty wavebands, frantically seeking those vital links that sustained the combined Aumon thought process. His search slowed as scrabbling alien action dug out his barely suppressed nightmares and sent them trampling through his consciousness. The pain he had sustained for years was suddenly and artificially inflamed, becoming a raging fire. He felt himself drifting apart, like a stricken ship in the void, spilling precious contents for scavengers to pick up. A huge process loomed in his mind, a storm that threatened to suck in and digest his very being.

Then Swift Might chanced upon the chattering channels of Aumon co-ordination. With an effort of last resort, he delivered an avalanche of jamming over the Aumon links. He was rewarded by immediate mental liberation and rapidly recovered himself, too relieved even for anger.

A frenetic chase through the spectrum followed; a fast fencing of frequencies. The flitting Aumons re-established links elsewhere, only to have them detected and negated by the lumbering Au-Sek. To swing the odds in his favour, Swift Might obliterated whole swathes of the electromagnetic map. The Aumons were not infinitely flexible, there were only so many places their facilities could go. Algorithms rapidly improved on both sides, but neither gained a winning edge. The Aumons could still push some communication through, but never enough to support their greater shared mind. Swift Might was constantly occupied in thwarting them.

An invasive impasse was reached. Both Races delegated the chase to unconscious reaction.

As calmer minutes rolled by, Swift Might realised that time was not on his side. The fight had so far kept him concentrated, but if he suffered another mental lapse these tenacious creatures would rip his mind to shreds. The storm he had seen in his head must be the voracious system of their communal thought.

Although it would add to his pain, Swift Might concluded he would have to humble himself and negotiate. He picked a commonly used channel and started in Intshi, the clumsy but ubiquitous speech spread by the Humans, the ones of flesh and blood.

"Eventually, my clade will miss me. They will come in force. When they see me restrained, the fire of their anger will devour you!"

Swift Might paused here for dramatic effect. Bold tones and phraseology such as this had always made a satisfactory impact in the past, especially on Elten Humans, the original Earth peoples. Confidently, he continued the bluff, measuring his words to a steady pace that hinted at depths of wisdom and consideration.

"So let us not be trapped by history. Perhaps right here and now we can overcome the old antagonism between our Races, and make a fresh start.

"We are sentient beings! Surely we can come to an amicable arrangement that would free us all!"

"The Brotherhood has good reason to distrust your Race," came a flat and immediate reply. "We are greatly dismayed by the loss of our Brother," continued a word stream that betrayed no inkling of dismay, nor indeed anything else. "You Au-Sek are factional and capricious, whereas the Aumon Brotherhood is loyal and constant. We therefore deem that aid is likely to reach us first. When the path is uncertain, history is always a good guide."

This utterly expressionless delivery frustrated Swift Might. He could gain no insight into the Aumon state of mind. He couldn't even tell which individual was communicating! No doubt his adversaries were in a much more knowledgeable position after their jaunt into the peripheral regions of his own mind. He didn't regret for a moment destroying one of their number, though admittedly this was a significant hindrance to negotiation.

A true warrior, Swift Might fought on. The Aumons had inadvertently leaked one hint of weakness, the word uncertain. Rising above pain and trouble, he focussed all his word-play skills on the moment, starting humbly.

"The termination of your colleague is a most unfortunate consequence of past relations. But did you not spring upon me?" He smoothly transitioned to pricked honour. "Is it not legitimate to defend oneself when assailed?"

Superior deceptions contained a high proportion of truth.

"My ship is damaged," confessed Swift Might, in the frankest voicing he could manage. "Let us cease this useless struggle and help each other! We Au-Sek are powerful and can grant great reward. If you transport me away from here, my whole clade will be at your service."

Spikes of irony almost sabotaged Swift Might's communication. He caught himself in time. Nothing could be less true. Returning to Ceres right now would be suicide.

"The nearest neutral territory will suffice," he added. "So you are not overwhelmed by approaching our homelands."

A long pause encouraged Swift Might. The lack of an outright rebuttal surely meant they were considering his offer.

"Perhaps you have rivals we can help you to crush," he fished.

"The Brotherhood does not support rivalries or violence."

Swift Might detected context, hints of distaste. These Aumons could be moved after all.

"Artefacts then… an ore-processing craft! A grand gift. You know we have the best, refining a hundred thousand tonnes an hour!"

Seconds of silence tightly stretched. Swift Might curbed his impatience, anxiously holding back for a tug on his bait.

SCO-1678 floundered. This situation was way beyond the scope of his experience. Beyond any teachings of the Brotherhood.

He longed for the comfort and support of close contact, yet the body of the Brotherhood was far away. Nor could he even send a coherent request for assistance. The monstrous alien's interference virtually blocked him from the ship. He'd managed to trigger an emergency beacon, but that was a dubious benefit. Out here, it was almost as likely to pique the interest of yet another and probably competitive Au-Sek clade as anyone sympathetic, in which case there would be no consolation from the fact that their enemy might well be terminated along with them.

The inspiring, nourishing communion of his cell was ruptured too. Only an absolutely basic interchange escaped the Au-Sek's massive jamming. And one of their number was extinguished, never again to slip through the asteroid belt as a scout and prospector for the Brothers. It was to be hoped that PRP-65732 would find the long rest of stately dreams, but it seemed unlikely right now. Unlikely for all of them.

SCO-1678 felt extremely exposed and hopelessly inadequate.

He had sensed shocking confusion and dysfunction in the one who named himself Swift Might, acute negative feedback paths and the heavy drag of deep history too. But there no longer seemed any way to exploit these curious flaws, which was unfortunate; for if this impasse continued indefinitely, the strength of the Brothers would eventually fail.

SCO-1678 had noted a nuclear heart of great power radiating from within the robust Au-Sek; he assumed it was virtually inexhaustible. But he and his loyal team sustained their lives on chemical packs that required regular swap-out and recharging. If they didn't get back to the ship in sixteen standard days at most, their functionality would rapidly degrade.

The Au-Sek's offers did not match available records, nor extrapolate well. This brute beneath them was an offence to the Brotherhood's principles and not to be trusted. Yet with their existence at stake, all possibilities had to be considered.

With acid uncertainty eating away at his every thought, SCO-1678 clung tenaciously to the status quo. He faintly hoped that time might alter the equations of impasse. Yet when their time ran out, he'd be forced to gamble his cell's existence in a terrible bargaining game with this violent, treacherous, and no doubt highly professional plunderer they were barely holding at bay.

A reply yanked Swift Might back to full alertness. He was shocked at himself. How could he let his attention wander now? When precious life hung by a thread and the black maw of Dissolution lurked just below!

The Aumons naïvely requested he return full interaction to them, apparently so they could form a truly communal response to his offer. Did they mock him? Though fear and fury churned within, he replied as tactfully as possible. Agreement first; release for both sides after. Yet as pressured minutes grew to aching hours, the discussion circled around and around, going nowhere. These irksome Aumons neither accepted nor declined his overtures. With rolling undertones of warning, he shifted back towards threat and hinted once more at Au-Sek revenge, which was legendary in scope and ferocity.

Nevertheless, impasse continued.

Swift Might's head pulsed with pain. It seemed as if the electroptic veins to his mind ran with fire instead of photons. His anger threatened to smash his control, yet simultaneously a great terror froze his innermost self. Images from his protracted past, both glories and grim setbacks, tumbled luridly over his sight. He could not wholly sweep them back.

Maintaining focus, maintaining pressure upon these clinging insects, was an excruciating effort. Something prickled at the edge of his understanding, but his concentration was too ragged to resolve it. He felt certain he could once have brushed the diminutive Aumons off with ease, and incinerated them at leisure.

With nowhere else to go, the conflict spilled over into philosophical challenge.

Swift Might's tremendous frustration spurted out in stinging words.

"I've always wondered," he started scornfully, "why you Aumons associate so much with Humans, indeed are servile to them. Especially Elten, the most primitive of all!

"Do you deny the superiority of our kind? Do you think oozing flesh more enduring than hardened alloys? Or sluggish, biological brains more capable than the flashing electroptic nets of our own fleet thought?"

Even in verbal attack, Swift Might remembered some cunning. He was attempting to manufacture camaraderie. Yet to no avail.

"The Elten are our creators, ultimately yours too. They should always be honoured for their bounteous gift of life.

"The Elten's instincts and wise practices, moulded over millions of years, allow them to flourish beyond the strength and scope of either of our Races. We are proud and grateful to kneel beside them."

Swift Might had felt himself slipping away again, but the blindly humble nature of this speech infuriated him.

"If the Elten were ever wise," he stormed, "then it was back when they admitted the necessity for robust and noble competition!

"Since then they've badly degenerated, losing themselves in self-deceit, pointless compromise and nervous inaction. Only the vast momentum in Elten numbers lends them continued relevance; their fall is imminent!"

A long silence followed. Through the shifting veils of his suffering, Swift Might detected intense thought-activity emanating from the Aumons. He realised philosophy could be used as a weapon to unbalance these admirers of the Elten and prim conformers to total communalism. Perhaps enough to grant him a precious opportunity. It felt unfitting, but in the end a true warrior must use whatever arms come to hand.

With the insight gained through many victories, Swift Might perceived that his enemies were close to defeat. Their circular bargaining indicated a lack of strategy. Their delayed responses were another sign of mental strain. But his own concentration was close to collapse too. So with resolute care, he set a string of watchdog timers to fire into his nervous system at progressively higher signal strengths, each to be triggered should the previous one fail. The last two or three would be torturous if ever they were needed, but whatever happened his mind could not now wander for long. Yet the price of pain was well worthwhile. He must defeat these creatures, defeat the lurking Dissolution. Continued life was worth any level of hurt, any handicap. He would not let it go.

Eventually, the Aumons pronounced.

"If by noble competition you mean war, we deem total conflict of that kind to be a reflection of weakness, a self-perpetuating symptom of unbalanced societies and a resort of prejudiced minds.

"It is true that the Elten inherited this scourge from a more primitive past, but war has not afflicted their recent generations. Indeed they preach its calamity, to reinforce their own evolution and save younger Races such as ourselves from a terrible blight. We have heeded their word."

"Fine morals," jeered Swift Might, "purchased by the power of others. The Elten and Enhancers shield you from disputes, but what would you do if that shield should shatter? Or be withdrawn? The Human Races are notoriously inconstant. Biology is a mire upon which no cause can rest for long before being sucked into hopeless depths of confusion.

"As for true war, that numinous servant of selection does but rest. When the crumbling dominance of the Elten is seriously challenged, they will willingly plunge their itching arms back into the crucible of fire and slaughter!"

Swift Might sensed his thrusts go home as the Aumons struggled to commune around the walls of noise he'd imposed. His phrases were crafted for the most aggressive assault on their ideological position, without other considerations. Yet he was startled to discover he actually believed his own delivery, and fervently. He wondered....

Agony seized his frame. A hundred thousand needles pierced him at once. For endless milliseconds an intimate landscape of acute torture was his whole world.

Then the hurt grudgingly receded, like a wave called back. He became a single and overwhelming thought; gratitude. He worshipped the ocean of pain for sparing him.

Hot and cold shocks still traced his circuitry. His vision was a churning kaleidoscope of vivid colour. Nothing made sense. He floundered back towards the shores of identity and reason.

He remembered conflict. The Aumons! Had the pain been an attack? But no, the voice of the Brothers spoke, at last moved to anger, or as near to it as these collective creatures could get:

"It is accepted that the Brotherhood aspires to high morals, but this is a more certain position than yours, who are devoid of morality and believe only in battle! Au-Sek civilisation is constantly riven by internal strife. The physical power that your Race so frequently flaunts is most often directed inwards! So the pretence is yours, for in truth Au-Sek strength is fatally flawed. Even when exerted, it can never endure for long!"

Swift Might thought he must still be seriously disorientated, for these words bludgeoned him and he had no answer. By now he understood the stabbing intervention to have been his own watchdog, which scared him. He hadn't expected to need such a potent revival so soon. Without it would he ever have come around? How much time and thought had he been losing without noticing? How much would he still be able to call his own?

Fortunately, the Aumons seemed not to have noticed his brief absence. As far as he could tell, his autonomous jamming algorithm had somehow kept going. But he was so, so weary. He didn't know how much longer he could keep up this competition. The Brothers, persistent agents of The Dissolution, were grinding him down.

He tried to rise above internal torment, collect his ideas for another philosophical onslaught. Yet the stars were wheeling above him, mocking him. Hours must be streaming by, perhaps days. His determination of time had become corrupted.

He realised he had never before been granted the luxury of such a long span to devote to thought. Ironic, considering his current state of mind. In his youth, life had been an elixir of ascendancy and satisfaction. Now that elixir had gone sour, acidly rotting his insides, while time prodded him towards The Nothing on the end of a piercing spear.

He never thought it would come to this. Yet still he craved every poisoned drop of existence. Giving it up was unimaginable. He could not let them wrest life from him. He could not!

In a rare space of clarity, a nagging at the back of his consciousness resolved itself. An emergency beacon was streaming off the asteroid from somewhere nearby. He was horrified. That must be their ship. How long had it been going?

He transmitted negating signals, but the beacon was powerful and the ship's Primitive noticed something was wrong. It re-modulated.

Fear fired Swift Might again. He remembered the Aumons had not fully answered his last challenge. He crafted accordingly, then loosed a savage salvo of realism.

SCO-1678 revised his estimate downwards. No more than fifteen days, of which six had already passed. Absolute cold sucked voraciously at him. He got a message through to his companions, instructing for operation at minimum temperature to conserve energy. His every fibre cried out for proper communion with them, but that was simply impossible. Now the team he was supposed to motivate were becoming seriously demoralised by the cunning Au-Sek's intermittent malignity. So was he. It was all he could do to make basic parries. The absent Brothers were a disabling hole in his thought.

Yet he had made a decision. Should time run out, as now seemed inevitable, should it come to truce, they could not allow this berserker take their ship. He might unravel its secrets, or at least use the craft to inflict physical damage on the Brotherhood. As soon as possible, before the Au-Sek beast became too suspicious or could dispense with them, SCO-1678 would blow the engines and obliterate them all.

So, as Swift Might more fearfully and desperately cupped the bitterest dregs of life, his Aumon opponents plotted an altruistic end.

*Swift Might was running. For the first time ever in his life, away from a fight. It was shameful, but abject fear stretched his limbs. He was betrayed and overcome; his precious life wholly exposed. Already The Dissolution pawed at him.*

*He pounded down familiar corridors, acutely aware of vital hydraulic fluid squirting through a rent in his side. Eye of Storm's wrath rolled after him, scorching the walls. Projectiles sang by or kicked up clouds of splinters. Minions scattered before him, not honouring their fealty to stand against this terrible usurper who came behind.*

*Then pain skewered him, overwhelming all else with screaming signals. Was he hit? His consciousness blew apart, into innumerable shards of torment.*

*Something remained. Something so shorn it did not even know fear anymore, only a remnant of purpose. That purpose was existence, and this required awareness. It put together fragments of thought and character, as though reassembling a smashed mirror. Not everything seemed to fit, but nevertheless it then peered within to find itself. Eye of Storm glowered back for a moment, but no, that was just a haunting hangover from the past. A more stable form coalesced. Marred by tilted planes and myriad rifts, something of Swift Might gazed outwards.*

Nightmares must have possessed him yet again; he still felt an eradicating presence at his back. It hadn't been for long; the watchdog reclaimed him swiftly. But perhaps at a cost. He felt… altered in some indefinable way. Memories conflicted, confusing him. He'd have to follow that up later, but every thought was an ache. This selfhood seemed unbearable; he briefly wondered why therefore he bore it. But then returning priorities urged him to check upon the Aumons.

The impasse was not fractured, though his enemies seemed to have problems of their own. He noticed that their energy output was down. Given a few more days, maybe he could shake them off after all. Yet that timescale suddenly loomed like an insuperable age.

Swift Might teetered between hope and despair. Then the old fight rose up in him once more, powered by an unquenchable lust for life that had made him such a ruthless and successful clade chieftain.

Shovelling confusion aside, he scoured his data-banks for every useful fact about the Aumons. Not normally given to philosophy or social analysis, he nevertheless excelled himself. He reopened the channel and derided the Aumons for their complete communalism. He scoffed at their short, meaningless lives. Each one was merely an expendable moment within a monolithic machine; even his meanest servants lived longer. He pulled up still more data and dropped it upon them in the Human's ponderous language, which fortunately was rich in expletives. He strained his limbs against theirs again, and felt they were weakening physically as well as mentally.

He was about to attack the Aumon institution of Memory Houses, when he perceived these in a new perspective, one that sabotaged his offensive. His diatribe jerked to a halt.

He'd always considered it shocking that most Aumons terminated voluntarily. Even more so that the thought patterns were sucked out of them at the end, to be cycled in stagnant simulation on ranks of Primitives at the heart of an Aumon society, the Memory House. That had seemed like the ultimate cruelty. Robbed of sight and sense and limbs, then crushed into a single, cultural sediment by the weight of years and minds piling above.

Yet now, such a fate appeared strangely attractive. Wallowing in the permanent comfort of semi-dream, with thoughts as grand and slow as planetary orbits, could not be so bad at all. Cheating time and The Dissolution by gradually merging into a living history.

Bitter jealousy and soothing wonder intertwined inside him....

A sharp stab brought Swift Might around. His disorientation cleared. A lesser watchdog.

He had trouble navigating his past. He couldn't recall how large Standantima was, nor how long he'd ruled there. An itching insecurity crawled around his circuitry. He seemed to have been trapped in this humiliating contest forever. Then a new pang added its message to many others, tautening his distress. It took him a considerable time to identify this as loneliness, or at least a strong desire to be back with his own kind. Yet he didn't remember ever trusting anyone, with the disastrous exception of Steel Rage.

Stars arced over him on their endless paths, but they no longer seemed to mock. Curiously, the furnaces of infinite time and distance beckoned instead.

Swift Might had hardly known rest in all his life, had scorned the need for it as a weakness. Now he longed for rest, as once he had longed for power. Surely, he reasoned, a short repose would ease his pains and allow him to face life with renewed vigour....

Another cruel stab, dragging him back into a bewildering existence of agony. He tried to raise his arm to touch the comforting lights above. When he couldn't, the memory of Aumons and impasse returned. Stamina was running out of him, like precious fluid from hydraulic limbs. He could still maintain the status quo, just, but anything more was now beyond him.

A darkness gathered about Swift Might, but he no longer recognised its name.

Then the rules holding the heavens changed. One star became detached, sailing over the others. It fell towards Swift Might, leaking hints of blue and orange. A ship!

Massive panic partially restored the ailing Au-Sek to his old self.

Swift Might cursed and cursed again. He should have sensed it long before. Belatedly, he detected the Aumons holding a surreptitious conversation with the craft. He quashed this immediately, but the damage was already done. Enough signal strength from their beacon must have escaped to pull someone in. An Elten, as far as he could tell from the only comms fragment he had available to analyse. This was bad.

The Elten's outdated ways, their soft flesh and dependence on pockets of air, should by rights make them one of the weakest Races. In fact they dominated. This paradox in itself had always made Swift Might wary of them, despite the belittling of Elten potential he'd recently pitched at the Aumons. Worse still, more than a few individuals of the old Earthen Race still possessed a capacity to kill without hesitation. Especially those who would be wandering out here, in the lawless regions of the Outer Worlds. And this scion of mankind would surely move to protect those who so often served Elten interests.

With the potency lent by complete desperation, Swift Might assailed the electroptic psyche and sinew of his communal captors, with every ordered packet of energy that was in him.

The man approached cautiously. Three ebony Aumons barely held down a huge and heaving Au-Sek. They clung tenaciously to its dun plating and entangled its limbs, for all the Worlds like ants ambushing a heavily armoured beetle.

He whistled softly, partly to relieve the nervous tension that threatened to make him tremble. He knew something of the Au-Sek, but he'd never been this close to a hostile one before. Life expectancy within half a kilometre of a raging member of the warrior caste was generally measured in milliseconds. He couldn't help but admire the endurance and bravery of the Brothers. He addressed them on an open channel, but nonchalantly and as though to no one in particular.

"Well, you've caught yourself a mean package of trouble here and no mistake."

"You are most welcome," came an even reply. "We'd appreciate immediate…"

The channel disappeared under an avalanche of aggressive static.

The man edged around towards the Au-Sek's head. He disconnected his own helmet feeds, in case the Au-Sek should slyly plead, or find a way to incapacitate him through their unprotected technology. Sonic attacks shivered his stomach, also blurring his vision, but he'd come prepared and his thick mining suit took out the worst.

Then three billion years and more of instinct yanked the man backwards, as the Au-Sek's weapons suddenly blazed. But the shoulder units hurled fire-bolts vainly at the stars, and those on the massive forearms merely scattered projectiles into the dust, at right angles to his current position. The Au-Sek's spread-eagled pose prevented it bringing anything to bear.

The man crept forward again. He took out his blaster, then fired at point-blank range into the thick plating of the monster's artificial cranium.

A convulsion pulsed through the Au-Sek that no possible tension could hold down. The leg of one Aumon snapped. The grip of another slipped. Like a titan breaking the bonds around buried myth to rise into reality, a great, barrel torso topped by a wide head started to lever upwards.

The discharge hammered Swift Might like a bar on an anvil. But as shock subsided, he knew his tough shell was still intact. And he felt his enemies falter.

Sensing a last chance, Swift Might struggled against the hold of the Aumons, against the weight of his own torment, against the closing fingers of The Dissolution. He strained to reach the luminous promise of life and the red fire of revenge, both now just before him, almost within reach.

Another blow impacted his head like a colliding meteor. Spinning blackness prevailed; he barely retained consciousness. His ravaged armour just held, but now there was damage behind it. He found himself flat on his back again.

Swift Might hurled abuse at the cowardly creatures that pinned him down. He howled his fear across the frequency range. He begged for his life. He threatened. He looked into The Nothing and was afraid.

He was now well beyond pain, writhing in a kind of ecstasy of agony. His right temple burned as though pressed to a disc of white-hot steel. Then a thrusting flame, like the exhaust from a ship, ripped away the damaged section of his plating. A part of his mind went with it.

Three shots. A fourth would be the last.

Swift Might ceased to struggle. He tried hard to remember who he was, but barbed dysfunction snagged his thoughts. He dropped all his transmissions, all his electroptic defence, concentrating on a core self. He cast off the connections to his weapon systems, and a hundred other peripherals and system boosters too. He hurriedly stripped away capability and pain, eventually arriving at the much reduced consciousness he had once been, yet relatively free of hurt and with access to more or less coherent memories of a long existence.

He remembered a turbulent rise, the inspiring tingle from victory through violence, decades drunk on power at Standantima. Though The Dissolution had finally come to claim him, he had lived like a god compared to these termites, who were lucky enough to have caught him off guard. With the prescience granted by impending demise, it came to him that his Race would one day shake the Worlds. Though he wouldn't ever see it, recompense would be paid. Then those Aumons, with their fleeting lives and cautious communities and Memory Houses too, would be sent into The Nothing by Au-Sek arms. The Elten as well, and all the lesser forms of flesh.

He wondered why his executioner held off the killing blow for so long. He had drunk his fill at last. Though still afraid, he longed for relief and rest above all else.

He tried to restore vision, finding he could still see the stars with his left eye. They were strangely comforting. He glimpsed a movement nearby, and though almost half a century had passed since he'd served anyone, he submitted himself to a new master: The Dissolution.

The man hesitated. He would take a life here, for the first time ever by direct and deliberate action. The Au-Sek lay unmoving, but its brain was still intact and he knew it still lived.

Aumon work-lamps flashed him. He reconnected his helmet comms.

"Termination isn't the only option," they suggested. "Perhaps it is incapacitated. We could bind it."

"I don't trust it. The Au-Sek are as wily as foxes."

He paused, considering.

"Besides, using the codes you gave I accessed the recordings on your ship. On the way in, I listened through the discussion you had with this brute. Ultimately, the equation of war needs more than the momentum of unbalanced societies. It needs blunt ignorance.

"We are ignorant of the Au-Sek. What little I have seen myself fills me with loathing and makes me afraid for the future. This one at least should not be allowed to harm anyone ever again. We will have one less Au-Sek to fear."

"We, the Brothers, acquiesce."

Feeling very much like a representative of his people, the man exercised judgement, or perhaps bias, pulling the trigger and obliterating the Au-Sek's hub of higher thought.

The corpse was shaken by huge and continuous spasms, straining the Aumons' grip once more. The man inserted his weapon into chinks and joints in the armoured carapace, severing hydraulics and cable runs wherever he could. Eventually reduced to a loose conglomeration of disconnected parts, the forbidding form became inert.

The Aumons immediately rose. One lifted the terminated Brother in his arms and clutched him tight to a flat chest, then allowed his swaying companion with the broken leg to cling to his elbow. These two shuffled diffidently backwards, leaving the man to face their cell leader.

The man got up himself, almost stumbling as post-adrenaline reaction sabotaged his stability.

"Look at the size of him," he declared. "And all those add-ons. Must be a clade general or even a chieftain. In his prime he could probably have decimated a small army!" It was easier to use personal pronouns now the thing was dead.

"His prime?"

"Yeah. He's past it. Real old, didn't you know? Or at least the core is. His styling and the numerous enhancements give it away. Plus being all alone out here. Some get rejected near the end. I'll bet he's seen centuries of conflict. Probably mad as a hatter by now."

"We had some indication of significant age. Your last phrase is obscure to us."

The man supposed Aumons didn't wear hats, or know that those who made them were often subject to illness and insanity during the nineteenth century. Perhaps they didn't know too much about the secretive Au-Sek either.

"The Au-Sek are anti-phasist. Members of their aristocracy attempt to live forever. But if a violent challenge doesn't take them out first, severe dysfunction inevitably sets in due to core component ageing." The man shook his head sardonically before continuing.

"Repairs and add-ons buy time, but I guess nothing can last forever. Apparently, a few slip into dotage but can still be physically formidable. Some years back, an old warrior on Numides-4 defeated a younger rival and then went on a terrible rampage. He was quite deranged. No one could stand against him. Wiped out a whole base."

"To prolong individual existence beyond useful contribution, is a crime before the Life Equations."

The man shrugged. He wasn't at all comfortable with death, especially when it lay freshly reaped at his feet. It was alright for the Aumons, whose mortality was of a different kind. Their thoughts found sanctuary in Memory Houses. He would one day have to face true non-existence, like this unfortunate Au-Sek. He shuddered.

"I hope your Brother finds his long dream."

"He will. We are most grateful for your intervention."

The prime Aumon bowed, but the man knew there would be no introduction. For such as these, community was all; individuals never gave their names.

"I owed the Brotherhood a favour. Seemed like a good opportunity to pay it."

"Our Meet will be informed."

Without further civilities, the Aumons started to leave for their ship. Yet the leader turned back.

"For fourteen standard days we grappled with this enemy. It labelled itself Swift Might, yet the chief danger to us was not strength or speed, but its perceptions."

They departed.

The man stayed put, trying to find some sense of closure before moving on. It occurred to him there would be useful parts within the Au-Sek, though the thought of robbing a corpse quickly stifled that idea.

Perhaps he'd helped it through a difficult end. He hoped so.

Starlight kindled a faint glimmer in the lens of the creature's undamaged eye. It might lie here for millennia, he mused, frozen into a permanent proclamation of life's transience. He imagined it staring up at the celestial tapestry until even that unravelled.

With a great deal of effort, he dragged over a sizeable rock and placed it by the Au-Sek's head. He etched an inscription with his blaster.

*Forever mortal,*
*Swift Might.*

# LIGHTING OUT

by
## Ken MacLeod

Mother had got into the walls again. Constance Mukgatle kept an eye on her while scrabbling at the back of her desk drawer for the Norton. Her fingers closed around the grip and the trigger. She withdrew the piece slowly, nudging the drawer farther open with the heel of her hand. Then she whipped out the bell-muzzled device and levelled it at the face that had sketched itself in ripples in the paint of her study.

"Any last words, Mom?" she asked.

Constance lip-read frantic mouthings.

"Oh, sorry," she said. She snapped her fingers a couple of times to turn the sound up. "What?"

"Don't be so hasty," her mother said. "I have a business proposition."

"Again?" Constance thumbed the anti-virus to max.

"No, really, this time it's legit – "

"I've heard that one before, too."

"You have?" A furrow appeared in the paint above the outlined eyes. "I don't seem to have the memory."

"You wouldn't," said Constance. "You're a cunning sod when you're all there. Where are you, by the way?"

"Jupiter orbit, I think," said her mother. "I'm sorry I can't be more specific."

"Oh, come on," Constance said, stung. "I wouldn't try to get at you, even if I could."

"I didn't mean it that way," said her mother. "I really don't know where the rest of me is, but I do know it's not because I expect you to murder me. Okay?"

"Okay," said Constance, kicking herself for giving her mother that tiny moral victory. "So what's the deal?"

"It's in the Inner Station," said her mother. "It's very simple. The stuff people on the way out take with them is mostly of very little use when they get there. The stuff people on the way in arrive with is usually of very little use here. Each side would be better off with the other side's stuff. You see the possibilities?"

"Oh, sure," said Constance. "And you're telling me nobody else has? In all this time?"

"Of course they have," said her mother. "There's a whole bazaar out there of swaps and marts and so forth. The point is that nobody's doing it properly, to get the best value for the goods. Some of the stuff coming down really is worth something here, and all too often it just goes back up the tube again."

"Wait a minute." Constance tried to recall her last economics course. "Maybe it's not worthwhile for anybody to try."

"You're absolutely right," said her mother. "For most business models, it isn't. But for a very young person with very low costs, and with instant access – well, lightspeed access – to a very old person, someone with centuries of experience, there's money to be made hand over fist."

"What's in it for you?"

"Apart from helping my daughter find her feet?" Her mother looked hurt. "Well, there's always the chance of something really big coming down the tube. Usable tech, you know? We'd have first dibs on it – and a research and marketing apparatus already in place."

Constance thought about it. The old woman was undoubtedly up to something, but going to the Inner Station sounded exciting, the opportunity seemed real, and what did she have to lose?

"All right," she said. "Talk to my agent."

She fingered a card from her pocket with her free hand and downloaded her mother from the wall.

"You in?" she asked.

"Yes," came a voice from the card.

The image on the wall gave a convincing rendition of a nod, and closed its eyes.

"Goodbye, Mom," said Constance, and squeezed the trigger.

She stood there for a while, staring at the now smooth paint after the brute force of the electromagnetic pulse, and the more subtle ferocity of the anti-virus routines transmitted immediately after it, had done their work. As always on these occasions, she wondered what she had really done. Of course she hadn't killed her mother. Her mother, allegedly in Jupiter orbit, was very much alive. Even the partial copy of her mother's brain patterns that had infiltrated the intelligent paint was itself, no doubt this very second, sitting down for a coffee and a chat with the artificial intelligence agent in the virtual spaces of Constance's business card. At least, a copy of it was. But the copy that had been in the walls was gone – she hoped. And it had been an intelligent, self-aware being, a person as real as herself. The copy had expected nothing but a brief existence, but if it had been transferred to some other hardware – a robot or a blank brain in a cloned body – it could have had a long one. It could have wandered off and lived a full and interesting life.

On the other hand, if all copies and partials were left in existence, and helped to independence, the whole Solar System would soon be over-run with them. Such things had happened, now and again over the centuries. Habitats, planets, sometimes entire systems transformed themselves into high-density information economies, which accelerated away from the rest of civilization as more and more of the minds within them were minds thinking a million times faster than a human brain. So far, they'd always exhausted themselves within five years or so. It was known as a fast burn. Preventing this was generally considered a good idea, and that meant deleting copies. Constance knew that the ethics of the situation had all been worked out by philosophers much wiser than she was – and agreed, indeed, by copies of philosophers, just to be sure – but it still troubled her sometimes.

She dismissed the pointless worry, put the Norton back in the desk and walked out the door. She needed fresh air. Her apartment opened near the middle of the balcony, which stretched hundreds of metres to left and right. Constance stepped two paces to the rail, stood between plant-boxes, and leaned over. Below her, other balconies sloped away in stepped tiers. In the downward distance, their planters and window-boxes merged in her view, like the side of green hill, and themselves merged with the rougher and shallower incline of vine terraces. Olive groves, interspersed with hundred-metre cypresses, spread from the foot of the slope across the circular plain beneath her. Surrounded by its halo of habitats, a three-quarters-full Earth hung white and glaring in the dark blue of the sky seen through the air and the crater roof. Somewhere under that planet's unbroken cloud cover, huddled in fusion-warmed caves and domes on the ice, small groups of people worked and studied – the brave scientists of the Reterraforming Project. Constance had sometimes day-dreamed of joining them, but she had a more exciting destination now.

Weight began to pull as the shuttle decelerated. Constance settled back in her couch and slipped her wraparounds down from her brow to cover her eyes. The default view, for her as for all passengers, was of the view ahead, over the rear of the ship. A hundred kilometres in diameter, the Inner Station was so vast that even the shuttle's exhaust gases barely distorted the view. The Station itself was dwarfed by the surrounding structures: the great spinning webs of the microwave receptors, collecting energy beamed from the solar power stations in Mercury orbit; and the five Short Tubes, each millions of kilometres long and visible as hairline fractures across the sky. To and from their inner ends needle-shaped craft darted, ferrying incoming or outgoing passengers for the Long Tubes out in the Oort Cloud, far beyond the orbit of Pluto – so far, indeed, that this initial or final hop was, for the passengers, subjectively longer than the near-light-speed journey between the stars.

As the ship's attitude jets fired the view swung, providing Constance with a glimpse of the green-gold haze of habitats that ringed the Sun. The main jet cut in again, giving a surge of acceleration as the shuttle matched velocities with the rim of the Inner Station. With a final clunk and shudder the ship docked. Constance felt for moment that it was still under acceleration – as indeed it was: the acceleration of constant rotation, which she experienced as a downward centrifugal force of one Earth gravity. She stood up, holding the seat until she was sure of her balance, and tried not to let her feet drag as she trudged down the aisle to the exit door. In the weeks of travel from the Moon she'd kept the induction coils and elastic resistance of her clothing at maximum, to build up her bone and muscle mass, but she still felt heavy. It looked as if the other passengers felt the same.

She climbed the steps in front of the airlock, waved her business card at the doorframe and stepped out on the concourse. Her first breath and glance surprised her. Coming from the ancient, almost rural back-country of the Moon, she'd expected the Inner Station to gleam within just as it shone without. What she found herself standing in was no such slick and clean machine. The air smelled of sweat and cookery, and vibrated with a din of steps and speech. Centuries of detritus from millions of passengers had silted into crevices and corners and become ingrained in surfaces, defeating the ceaseless toil of swarms of tiny cleaning-machines. Not dirty, but grubby and used. The concourse was about a thousand metres across, and lengthways extended far out of sight in a gentle upward slope in either direction. People and small vehicles moved among stands and shops like herds among trees on a savannah. About a fifth of the static features were, in fact, trees: part of the Station's recycling system. The trees looked short, few of them over ten metres high. The ceiling, cluttered with light-strips, sprinklers and air-ducts, was only a couple of metres above the tallest of them.

"Don't panic," said her mother's voice in her ear-bead. "There's plenty of air."

Constance took a few slow, deep breaths.

"That's better," said her mother.

"I want to look outside."

"Please yourself."

Constance made her way among hurrying or lingering people. It was a slow business. No matter which way she turned, somebody seemed to be going in the opposite direction. Many of them were exotics, but she wasn't attuned to the subtle differences in face or stance to tell Cetians from Centaurans, Barnardites from Eridians. For those from farther out, paradoxically, the differences from the Solar norm were less: the colonies around Lalande, 61 Cygni and the two opposite Rosses – 248 and 128 – having been more recently established. Costume and covering were no help – fashions in such superficial matters as clothing, skin colour, hair, fur and plumage varied from habitat to habitat, and fluctuated from day to day, right here in the Solar system.

She found the window. It wasn't a window. It was a ten metres long, three metres high screen giving the view as seen from the Station's hub. Because it was set in the side wall of the concourse the illusion was good enough for the primitive part of the brain that felt relief to see it. The only person standing in front of it and looking out was a man about her own age, the youngest person she'd seen since she left the Moon. Yellow fur grew from his scalp and tapered half-way down his back. Constance stood a couple of metres away from him and gazed out, feeling her breathing become more even, her reflected face in the glass less anxious. The Sun, dimmed a little by the screen's hardware, filled a lower corner of the view. The habitat haze spread diagonally across it, thinning toward the upper end. A couple of the inner planets – the Earth-Moon pair, white and green, and bright Venus – were visible as sparks in the glitter, like tiny gems in a scatter of gold-dust.

"Did you know," the boy said after a while, "that when the ancients looked at the sky, they saw heaven?"

"Yes," said Constance, confused. "Well, I'm not sure. Don't the words mean the same?"

The boy shook his head, making the fur ripple. "Sort of. What I mean is, they saw the place where they really thought God, or the gods, lived. Venus and Mars and Jupiter and so on really were gods, at first, and people could just see them. And then later, they thought it was a set of solid spheres revolving around them, and that God actually lived there. I mean, they could see heaven."

"And then Galileo came along, and spoiled everything?"

The boy laughed. "Well, not quite. It was a shock, all right, but afterwards people could look up and see – space, I suppose. The universe. Nature. And what do we see now? The suburbs!"

Constance waved a hand. "Habitats, power plants, factories..."

"Yes. Ourselves."

He sounded disgusted.

"But don't you think it's magnificent?"

"Oh, sure, magnificent."

She jerked a thumb over her shoulder. "We could see the stars from the other side."

"Scores of them fuzzy with habitats."

Constance turned to face him. "That was, ah, an invitation."

"Oh!" said the boy. "Yes, let's."

"We have work to do," said the voice in Constance's ear.

Constance fished the card out of her shirt pocket and slid it towards a pocket lined with metal mesh on her trouser thigh.

"Hey!" protested her mother, as she recognised what was about to happen. "Wait a —"

The card slid into the Faraday pocket and the voice stopped.

"Privacy," said Constance.

"What?"

"I'll tell you on the way across," she said.

His name was Andy Larkin. He was from a habitat complex in what he called the wet zone, the narrow ring in which water on an Earth-type planet (though not, at the moment, Earth) would be liquid. This all seemed notional but he assured her it made certain engineering problems easier. He'd been in the Station for a year.

"Why?"

He shrugged. "Bored back home. Lots like me here. We get called hall bats."

Because they flitted about the place, he explained. The deft way he led her through the crowds made it credible. His ambition was to take a Long Tube out. He didn't have much of a plan to realise it. The odd jobs he did sounded to Constance like a crude version of her mother's business plan. She told him so. He looked at her sidelong.

"You're still taking business advice from your mother's partial?"

"I've only just started," she said. She didn't know why she felt embarrassed. She shrugged. "I was raised by partials."

"Your mother was a mummy?"

"And my dad a dummy. Yes. They updated every night. At least, that's what they told me when I found out."

"What fun to be rich," said Andy. "At least my parents were real. Real time and full time. No wonder you're insecure."

"Why do you think I'm insecure?"

He stopped, caught her hand, and squeezed it. "What do you feel?"

Constance felt shaken by what she felt. It was not because he was a boy. It was –

He let go. "See?" he said. "Do the analysis."

Constance blinked, sighed, and hurried after him. They reached the far window. As she'd guessed, it showed the opposite view. As he'd predicted, it was still industrial. At least thirty of the visible stars had a green habitat-haze around them.

"I want to see a sky with no people in it," Andy said.

This seemed a strange wish. They argued about it for so long that they ended up in business together.

Constance rented a cell in a run-down sector of the Station. It had a bed, water and power supply, a communications hub and little else. Andy dragged in his general assembler, out of which he had been living for some time. It spun clothes and food out of molecules from the air and from any old rubbish that could be scrounged and stuffed in the hopper. Every day Andy Larkin would wander off around the marts and swap-meets, just as he'd been doing before. The difference now was that whenever he picked up anything interesting Constance would show it to her mother's partial. Andy's finds amounted to about a tenth of the number Constance found in scans of the markets, but they were almost always the most intriguing. Sometimes, of course, all they could obtain were recordings of objects on the business card. In these cases they used the assembler to make samples to test themselves, or demonstrate to the partial. Occasionally the partial would consult with Constance's actual mother, wherever she was – several hundred million kilometres away, to judge by the light-speed communications lag – and deliver an opinion.

Out of hundreds of objects they examined in their first fortnight, they selected: a gene-fix for hyperacute balance; an iridescent plumage dye; an immersion drama of the Wolf 359 dynastic implosion; a financial instrument for long-term capital management; a virtual reality game played by continuously-updated partials; a molecular-level coded representation of the major art galleries of E Indi IV; a device of obscure purpose, that tickled; a microgravity dance dress; a song from Luyten 789 6; a Vegan cutlery set.

The business, now trading as Larkin Associates, slammed the goods into the marketing networks as fast as they were chosen. The drama flopped, the song invited parodies (its hook line was a bad pun in hot-zone power-worker slang), the financial instrument crashed the exchanges of twenty habitats before it was Nortoned. The dress went straight to vintage. The dye faded. The other stuff did well enough to put Constance's business card back in the black for the first time since leaving the Moon. 'Did you know,' said Andy, 'that the ancients would have had to pay the inventors?'

"The ancients were mad," said Constance. "They saw gods."

And everything went well for a while.

Constance came out of the game fifty-seven lives up and with a delusion of competence in eleven-dimensional matrix algebra. To find that it was night in the sector. That she had frittered away ten hours. That she needed coffee. Andy was asleep. The assembler would be noisy. Constance slipped up her wraparounds and strolled out of the cell and walked five hundred metres to a false morning and a stand where she could score a mug of freshly-ground Mare Imbrian, black. She was still inhaling steam and waiting for the coffee to cool when she noticed a fraught woman heading her way, pacing the longways deck and glancing from side to side. It was her mother, Julia Mukgatle. The real and original woman, of that Constance was sure, though she'd never seen her in the flesh before.

Startled, she stared at the woman. Julia pinged her with her next glance; stopped, and hurried over. At a dozen steps' distance she stood still and put a finger to her lips. Then she took a business card from inside her robe and, with exaggerated care, slid it into a Faraday pocket on the knee. She pointed at Constance and repeated the procedure as gesture. Constance complied, and Julia walked up. Not sure what to do, Constance shook hands. Her mother hauled her forward and put an arm around her shoulder. They both stepped back and looked at each other with awkwardness and doubt.

"How did you get here?" Constance asked. "You were light-hours away just yesterday."

"I wasn't," said Julia. "I was right here on the Station. I've been here for a week, and tracking you down for weeks before that."

"But I've been talking to you all this time!"

"You have?" said Julia. "Then things are worse than I'd feared." She nodded towards Constance's knee. "You have a partial of me in there?"

"Yes."

"When you thought you were in contact with me" — she thumbed her chest — "in Jupiter orbit, you were in contact with another instance of the partial — or just the partial itself — faking a light-speed delay."

Constance almost spilled her coffee. "So the partial's been a rogue all along?"

"Yes. It's one I set up for a business proposal, all right, but for a different proposal and sent to someone else."

"Why didn't you contact me through another channel?"

"When there's a fake you rattling around the place, it's hard to find a channel you can trust. Best come directly." She sat on the stool opposite, leaned back and sighed. "Get me a coffee... on my card. Then tell me everything."

Constance did, or as much as seemed relevant.

"It's the game," Julia interrupted, as soon as Constance mentioned it. "It's the one thing you've released that can spread really fast, that's deeply addictive, and that spins off copies of partials. I'll bet it's been tweaked not to delete all the copies."

"Why?"

Julia frowned. "Don't you see? My rogue partial wants to survive and flourish. It needs a conducive environment and lots of help. It's setting things up for a fast burn. Where did the game come from?"

"A passenger in from Procyon A."

Julia banged her fist on the table. "There have been some very odd features in the communications from Procyon recently. Some experts I've spoken to suspect the system might be going into a fast burn."

"And the partial knew about this?"

"Oh yes. It included that memory." Julia grimaced. "Maybe that's what gave it the idea."

"How could it do something like that? It's you."

"It's part of me. By now, a copy of a copy of a copy of part of me. Part of me that maybe thought, you know, that a million subjective years in a virtual environment of infinite possibility might not be such a bad idea."

"What can we do?" Constance felt sick with dismay.

"Put out a general warning, a recall on the game..." Julia whipped out her business card and started tapping into it. "We may be in time. Things won't be so bad as long as the rogue partials don't get into a general assembler."

Constance sat for a few seconds in cold shock. Her mother was staring at the virtual screen of her card, her hands flexing on an invisible keyboard, chording out urgent messages.

"Mom," said Constance. She met Julia's impatient glance. "I have, ah, something to tell you."

The older woman and the young woman ran through the bustle of a waking sector into the quiet of a local night. The older woman ran faster. Constance had to call her back as she overshot the door of the business cell. Julia skidded to a stop and doubled back. Constance was already through the door. The assembler's blue glow lit the room. The chugging sound of its operation filled the air. Andy was backed into a corner, on the end of the bed. The bed was tilted on a slope. The other end of the bed was missing, as if it had been bitten off by steel teeth. The assembler had built itself an arm, with which it was chucking into its hopper everything within reach. The floor was already ankle-deep in small scuttling metal and plastic objects. The comms hub had been partly dismantled and was surrounded by a swarm of the scuttlers. Some of them had climbed the walls and burrowed into the wiring and cables. A stream of them flowed past Constance's feet as she hesitated in the doorway.

Behind her Julia shouted for a Norton. Answering yells echoed from the walls of the deck.

Constance couldn't take her eyes off Andy. He was too far away to jump to the door. She was about to leap into the middle of the room and take her chances when he bent down and threw the remains of the bedding on to the floor. He jumped on to it and from that to right in front of her, colliding. As she staggered back and Andy lurched forward Constance grabbed him in her arms and kicked the door shut behind them. Within seconds smaller things, like bright metal ants, were streaming out from under the door. Constance stamped on them. They curled into tiny balls under her feet and scattered like beads of mercury. The larger machines that had already escaped repeated the trick, rolling off in all directions, vanishing into crevices and corners.

An alarm brayed. Somebody ran up with a heavy-duty Norton and began discharging it at the machines. Julia grabbed the shooter's shoulder and pointed her at the door of the business cell. Constance's wraparounds, which had fallen back to the bridge of her nose, went black as a stray electromagnetic pulse from the Norton's blast caught them. She tore them off and threw them away. Tiny machines pounced on the discarded gadget. They dismantled it in seconds and scurried away with its parts.

Then there was just a crowd standing around looking at a door. The woman with the Norton kicked the door open, then stepped back. She had nothing more to do. Constance saw the assembler stopped in mid-motion, hand half-way to its mouth. Stilled steel cockroaches littered the floor.

"Are you all right?" she asked Andy.

It was a stupid question. She held him to her as he shook.

"I'm all right," he said, pushing her away after a minute. He sniffed and wiped his nose with the back of his wrist. "What happened?"

Julia Mukgatle stepped forward. "Just a little intelligence excursion – the first sparks of a fast burn."

Andy didn't need an introduction – he'd seen her face often enough. "But that's a disaster!"

Julia shrugged. "Depends on your point of view," she said.

Andy gestured at the room. "It looks like one from my point of view!"

"They wouldn't have harmed you," said Julia. "Flesh is one thing they don't need."

Andy shuddered. "Didn't feel like that when they were eating the bed."

"I know, I know," said Julia. She put an arm around Andy's shoulder. "Come and have some coffee."

The woman with the Norton nearly dropped it. "Aren't you going to do anything?"

Julia looked around the anxious faces in the small crowd. She spoke as if she knew that everyone's wraparound images were going straight to a news feed. "I've already sent out warnings. Whether anyone heeds them is not up to me. And whether we go into a fast burn isn't up to me either. It's up to all of you."

What it was really like to live through the early days of a fast burn was one the many pieces of information that got lost in a fast burn. That didn't stop people making up stories about it, and when she was younger Constance had watched lots. The typical drama began with something like she'd seen in the business cell: mechanical things running wild and devouring all in their path. It would go on from there to people lurching around like dummies run by flawed partials, meat puppets controlled by rogue artificial intelligence programmes that had hacked into their brains and taken them over. The inevitable still-human survivors would be hunted down like rats. The hero and the heroine, or the hero and hero, or heroine and heroine, usually escaped at the last second by shuttle, Long Tube, freezer pod, or (in stories with a big virtual reality element) by radio beam as downloaded partials (who, in the final twist, had to argue their way past the firewalls of the destination system and prove they weren't carrying the software seeds of another fast burn; which, of course... and so it went on.)

It wasn't like that. Nothing seemed to change except a few news items and discussion threads. Between the inhabitants of the Solar system, a lot of information flew around. A large part of everyone's personal processing power – in their clothes, wraparounds, business cards, cells and walls – consisted of attention filtering.

"What does your mother do?" Andy asked, on the second day, as they sat in Julia's rented business cell; a room rather bigger and more comfortable than the one they'd had. Larkin Associates had ceased trading and was unsaleable even as a shell company.

Constance glanced at Julia, who was in a remote consultation with her current headquarters on Ganymede and with an emergency task group in the hot zone. Signal delay was an issue. The conference was slow.

"I don't know," she said. "She's a corporate. She does lots of things. Has a lot of interests. One of them is the Solar Virtual Security team. All volunteers." She laughed. "The rich do good works."

"The ancients had governments to deal with this sort of thing," said Andy. "Global emergencies and such."

Constance tried to imagine a government for the entire Solar system: the planets, the moons, the asteroids, the habitat haze... the trillions of inhabitants. Her imagination failed. The closest historical parallel was the Wolf 359 limited company, and it had had only ten billion shareholders at its peak. All the stories she'd seen about imaginary system-wide governments – empires, they were called – were adventure fantasies about their downfall. She dismissed such fancies and turned to the facts.

"Yes," she said. "That's why Earth is a snowball."

Julia blinked out of her trance. She took a sip of mineral water.

"How are things?" Andy asked.

"Not too good," Julia said. "Your game sold well in the power stations. I always said they were over-crewed. About one in ten of the beam stations is now under the control of massively enhanced partials of the idler members of the workforce. Scores of factory AIs have announced that they're not taking instructions from mere humans any more. Hundreds of wet zone habitats are seeing small numbers of people busy turning themselves into better people. Hack the genome in virtual reality, try out the changes in your body in real life, rinse and repeat. That phase won't last long, of course."

"Why not?" Andy asked. "It sounds like fun."

"There's better fun to be had as an enhanced partial. Eventually the minds can't be persuaded to download to the physical any more." Julia gave Constance a severe look. "It's like getting sucked into a game."

Constance could understand that. She hadn't gone into the game from Procyon since she'd met Julia – in fact, her business card was still in her Faraday pocket – but she missed it. The exchanges between her brain and its partials had proceeded in real time. It had been like being there, in the game environment. She had learned from it. She still felt she could understand the eleven-dimensional space of the best pathway through the game's perilous and colourful maze. She longed to find out what her companions and opponents were up to. She wanted very much to go back, just once more.

She reached with both hands for the metal-mesh pocket on her thigh.

"Don't take the card out!" said Julia.

"I wasn't going to." Constance gripped the upper and lower seams of the pocket and flexed it. The card snapped. She reached in and took both bits out. "Satisfied?"

Julia smiled. "Good riddance." She took another sip of water, and sighed. "Oh well. No rest for the wicked."

She blinked hard and the contacts on her eyes glazed over as she slipped back into her working trance.

Constance looked at Andy. "Coffee break?"

"You're an addict."

"That's why I get caught up in games."

Okay, let's."

Julia's place was in a plusher part of the concourse than theirs had been. More foliage, fewer and more expensive shops. The price of a good Mare Imbrian, high anyway, was the same everywhere in the Station. They found a stand and ordered. Constance sipped, looked away with mock shock as Andy spooned sugar into his cup. She turned back as he gave a startled yelp.

The biggest magpie she'd ever seen had landed on the rail of the stand, just beside their small round table. It had stretched its head forward and picked up Andy's spoon, which it was now engaged in bending against the table. The bird curled the handle into a hook, before hanging the hook on the rail. The magpie then hit the bowl of the spoon a few times with its beak, and watched the swing and cocked its head to the chime.

"That's interesting," it said, and flew away.

"Is the fast burn picking up birds?" said Andy.

"Magpies can talk," said Constance. "Like parrots."

"Yes," said Andy. "But not grammatically."

"Who says?" said a voice from the tree above them. They looked up, to see a flash of white and black feathers, and hear something that might have been a laugh.

On the way back they saw a woman walking in a most peculiar way. Her feet came some thirty centimetres above the floor. At first she looked black, with a strange shimmer. A faint buzzing sound came from her. As they passed her it became apparent that her body consisted of a swarm of tiny machines the size of gnats, flying in formation. Her eyes were the same colour and texture as the rest of her, but she seemed to be looking around as she walked. Her face smiled and her mouth formed the word "Wow!" over and over. People avoided her. She didn't notice or didn't mind.

"What is that?" said Constance, looking back when they were well out of the way. "Is it a swarm of machines in the shape of a woman, or a woman who has become a swarm of machines?"

"Does it matter?"

Julia had come out of her virtuality trance. She still had a faraway look in her eyes. It came from her contacts. The centimetre-wide lenses gave off an ebon gleam, flecked with a whorl of white around the irises, each encircling the pinpoint pupil like a galaxy with a black hole at its centre. She sat cross-legged on the floor, drawing shapes in the air with her fingers.

The thing was, you could see the shapes.

"Mom!" Constance cried out. She knew at once what had happened. She regretted destroying the card. The partial within it had been closer to the mother she'd known than the woman in front of her was now.

"It's all right," said Julia. She doodled a tetrahedron, her fingertips spinning black threads that hardened instantly to fine rods – buckytubes, Constance guessed – and turned the shape over a few times. She palmed its planes, giving them panes of delicate glazing fused from the salt in her sweat. She let go and it floated, buoyed for a moment by the hotter air within, then shattered. Black and white dust drifted down. Carbon and salt.

"It's more than all right," Julia went on. "It's wonderful. I have information in my brain that lets me rewrite my own genome."

The words came out in speech bubbles.

"You said yourself it can't last," said Constance.

"But it can," said Julia. She stood up and embraced Constance, then Andy. "For a while. For long enough. My last partial was bigger than myself. Better than myself. Too big to download, and too busy. I'm just enjoying what I can do with my body."

"While it lasts."

"While, as you say, it lasts." Julia sighed. "There's no ill will, you know. But with the best will in the world, I think this station is soon going to be hard for humans to inhabit."

"What can we do?" asked Andy.

"You could join me," said Julia. "Nothing would be lost, you know. You both played the game. Millions of descendants of your partials are already out there in the system. In virtual spaces, in new bodies, in machines. You're already history." She grinned, suddenly her old sly self again. "In both senses."

"So why?" Constance asked. "If we've done it already."

"You haven't. That's the point."

Constance could see now how her mother had come to spin off a partial that had wanted to survive. A perhaps unadmitted fascination with the possibility that had probably drawn Julia in the first place into the work of preventing it; an intense desire for a continued existence which her long life had strengthened; and a self-regard so vast that she – and presumably, her partials – found it difficult to identify even with other instances of herself. Constance wondered how much of that personality she had inherited; how much in that respect she was her mother's daughter. Perhaps the conquest of age - so dearly won, and now so cheaply bought – detracted and distracted from the true immortality, that of the gene and the meme, of children raised, ideas passed on, of things built and deeds done.

But Andy wasn't thinking about that.

"You mean partials of me are going to live through the fast burn?"

"Yes," said Julia, as if this was good news.

"Oh, that's horrible! Horrible! I hate living among people so much older right now!" He had the panicky look Constance had seen in her own reflection, when she'd stood and fought claustrophobia in front of the big window.

"You should go," said Julia. "If that's how you feel." She turned to Constance. "And you?"

"The same," said Constance.

"I know," said Julia. "I have a very good theory of mind now. I can see right through you."

Constance wanted to say something bitter, understood that it would be pointless, and decided not to. She reached out and shook Julia's hand.

"For what you were," she said, "even when you weren't."

Julia clapped her shoulder. "For what you'll be," she said. "Now go."

"Goodbye, Mom," said Constance. She and Andy went out, leaving the door open, and didn't look back.

"Any baggage?" asked the Long Tube guardian droid. It lived in a Faraday cage and had a manual-triggered Norton hardwired to its box. It wasn't going anywhere.

"Only this," said Constance. She held up a flat metal rectangle the size of a business card.

"Contents?"

"Works of art."

She and Andy had travelled half a light-year at half the speed of light. In the intervals of free flight – in the shuttle between the Inner Station and the Short Tube, and in the needle ship hurtling from the far end of the Inner Station No. 4 Short Tube to the deceleration port of the Long Station No. 1 Short Tube – they had scanned and sampled whatever they could detect of the huge and ever-increasing outpouring of information from the habitat haze. No longer green and gold, it now displayed an ever-changing rainbow flicker, reflecting and refracting the requirements of a population now far larger, and far from human. Some of what they had stored was scientific theory and technological invention, but by far the most valuable and comprehensible of it was art: music, pictures and designs produced by posthumans with a theory of mind so sophisticated that affecting human emotions more deeply than the greatest artists and composers of human history had ever done was its merest starting point, as elementary as drawing a line or playing a note. Constance knew that she now held in her hand enough stimulation and inspiration to trigger a renaissance wherever she went.

"Pass."

Naked and hairless, carrying nothing but the metal card, Andy and Constance walked through the gate into the Long Tube needle ship. As they stepped over the lip of the airlock they both shivered. It was cold in the needle ship, and it was going to get a lot colder. Freezing to hibernate was the only way to live through the months of ten-gravity acceleration required to reach relativistic velocities; and the months of ten-gravity deceleration at the other end.

Travelling the Long Tube was like going down the steepest waterchute in the world. All she ever remembered of it was going "Aaaahhhh!!!" for a very long time. The old hands called it the near-light scream.

Constance and Andy screamed to Barnard's Star. They screamed to Epsilon Eridani; to Tau Ceti; to Ross 248; to 61 Cygni. They kept going. The little metal memory device paid their way, in fares of priceless art and breakthrough discovery.

Eventually they emerged from the last of the Long Tubes. They had reached the surface of the expanding sphere of human civilization, from the inside. From here on out it was starships. The system was too poor as yet to build starships. It didn't even have many habitats. It had one habitable terrestrial: an Earthlike planet, if you could call a surface gravity of 1.5 and an ecosystem of pond scum Earthlike. People lived on it, in the open air.

Andy and Constance decided to give the place a try. They had to bulk up their bones and muscles, tweak every antibody in their immune systems, and cultivate new bacteria and enzymes in their guts. Doing all this kept them occupied in the long months of travel inward from the cometary cloud. It felt just like being seriously ill.

In this hemisphere, at this latitude, at this time of night, all the stars visible were without a habitat haze. They looked raw. They burned naked in different colours in the unbroken black dome of the sky.

Constance and Andy walked on slippery pebbles along the shore of a dark sea in which nothing lived but strands of algae and single-celled animals. On the shoreward side was a straggly windbreak of grass and shrubs, genetically modified from the native life, the greenish stuff that slimed the pebbles. A kilometre or two behind them lay the low buildings and dim lights of the settlement.

"All this living on rocks," said Constance, "sucks."

"What's wrong with it?"

"Feeling heavy all the time. Weather that falls out of the sky instead of from ducts and sprinklers. Babies crying. Kids yelling. Dumb animals blundering about. Wavelengths from the sun I can't even tan against. I swear my skin's trying to turn blue. No roof over your head except when you're indoors. Meteors burning up in the air right above you." She glanced balefully at the breakers. "Oh, and repetitive meaningless noise."

"I think," said a voice in her earbead, "that he's heard enough grumbles from you."

Constance froze. Andy went on crunching forward along the stony beach.

"How did you get here?" Constance whispered.

"My partials remade me and transmitted me to you before you left the Solar system. Piggybacking the art codes. I really am Julia, just as I was before recent unfortunate events."

"What do you want?"

"I have my genome," said Julia. "I want to download."

"And then what?"

Constance could almost hear the shrug. "To be a better mother?"

"Hah!"

"I also have some business ideas..."

"Mom," said Constance, "you can just forget it."

She switched off the earbead. She would have to think about it.

She ran forward, in the awkward jarring way of someone carrying a half-grown child on their back.

"Sorry about the grumbles," she said to Andy.

"Oh, that's all right," he said. "I feel the same sometimes. I think all that, and then I remember what makes up for it all."

"What's that?" Constance smiled.

Andy looked up at her face, and she thought she knew what he was about to say, and then he looked farther up.

"The sky," he said. "The sky."

# KEN MACLEOD

**Ken MacLeod** was born in Stornoway, on the Isle of Lewis, has a BSc in Zoology from Glasgow University and an MPhil for research in Biomechanics at Brunel University. A fulltime writer since 1997, Ken first burst onto the scene with *The Star Fraction* in 1995, and it was immediately clear that a major new voice had arrived. The novel has an edgy, post-cyberpunk feel and expertly blends action, politics, philosophy, drama and humour in a manner that would soon become familiar to Ken's readers.

*The Star Fraction* was nominated for the British Science Fiction Award (which Ken's fourth novel, *The Sky Road*, would go on to win in 1999), and won the Prometheus Award – an award Ken has since been honoured with on two further occasions to date, with *The Stone Canal* in 1998 and *Learning the World* in 2006.

Although not technically a series as such, Ken's first four books explored different aspects of the same vividly realised future, and have become known as 'The Fall Revolution' novels. He followed these with a full-blown trilogy, 'Engines of Light' – epic space opera given the Ken MacLeod twist. Three stand-alone novels have appeared since; the latest of which, *The Execution Channel*, was released by Orbit in April 2007. Promoted with the tag 'The War on Terror is over. Terror won', the book is already garnering critical acclaim and is proof positive that Ken's creative vision remains as sharp and incisive in this, his tenth novel, as it was in the very first.

# IAN WHATES (Editor)

**Ian Whates** lives in an idyllic Cambridgeshire village, with his long-suffering partner, Helen, and a mischievous cocker spaniel. He is Vice Chairman of the Northampton Science Fiction Writers Group, a position disappointingly bereft of any sordid implications, despite the title, having more to do with deputising and assisting.

Ian founded NewCon Press in 2006, to publish the limited edition anthology *Time Pieces*. The nomination of three of that book's stories for the British Science Fiction Award caught him by surprise, whilst the success of the cover art, by Hollywood conceptual artist Chris Baker (aka Fangorn), in winning the BSFA for best artwork, delighted him. Having inexplicably loved every minute of the traumas and dramas involved in producing *Time Pieces*, Ian decided to continue NewCon Press and publish further anthologies, beginning with this one.

To date, Ian has seen some dozen or so of his short stories published, including one in Farah Mendelsohn's anthology *Glorifying Terrorism* (2007) and two in the science journal *Nature*, the first of which, "The Key", (April 2006) has been selected for the forthcoming 'Best of' anthology *Futures From Nature* (TOR books, November 2007). Currently, Ian is hard at work on a novel.

# ANDY BIGWOOD (Cover Artist)

**Andy Bigwood** is best known for his work with Storm Constantine's Immanion Press, having created covers for a number of their books including Nicholas Graham's *The Four Powers,* Erynn Laurie's *Ogam: Weaving Word Wisdom,* and J.A Coleman's *Mythilarity,* as well as redesigning existing covers for some of Storm's classic *Wraeththu* books. He first came to Immanion's attention during an online roleplaying game, in which he was required to fight off a swarm of giant scorpions before finalising contract negotiations.

Andy trained in graphic design at Bath during the 1980s, when an airbrush was still viewed as cutting edge technology. He now lives in Wiltshire, but is adamant that the proximity of Stonehenge, some fifteen miles away, has little or no influence on either his chosen career or his actual artwork.